OPERATOR 5:
AMERICA'S PLAGUE BATTALIONS

SECRET SERVICE OPERATOR #5 ™

AMERICA'S UNDERCOVER ACE

AMERICA'S PLAGUE BATTALIONS

By Curtis Steele

STEEGER BOOKS • 2021

PROLOGUE

A MIGHTY flotilla of seaplanes lay in San Francisco Bay. Bobbing gently in the swell, these ships, with their synchronized machine guns and their underslung bomb racks, were potentially powerful weapons of war.

A big oil tanker was anchored in the bay off the Naval Training Station on Yerba Buena Island, and the planes in turn jockeying alongside to fill up with gasoline. The captain of the tanker supervised the servicing of a plane, then shouted down: "Sorry, but that's all the gas I got. I'm empty."

The pilots within hearing of his voice gazed at him blankly. Consternation spread among them, as they watched the tanker heave up its anchor and depart. Under the fifty huge arc lights that flooded the bay, their faces seemed suddenly drawn and despondent. They knew that, not so many miles to the east, a ruthless conqueror was marching across America. This was the fourth month of the Purple Invasion, and Rudolph I, Emperor of the Central Empire, had pushed back the American Defense Force almost to the Rocky Mountains—and in some cases beyond them.

Raiding airplanes of the Central Empire had flown as far as the west coast. Americans in conquered territory had been tortured and slaughtered in countless thousands. Civilian populations in many cities of the West had been infected with the bacteria of plague. America's one hope lay in this immense armada of seaplanes which had been manufactured in South America, and flown here. Thus far it had demonstrated its strength by destroying the Central Empire naval fleet. And

The Americans seemed possessed with a fanatical courage—charging directly into a withering hail of fire.

these aviators, every one dedicated to give his life in the defense of his country, were ready to fly against the enemy at once. But they could not fly without gasoline....

IN THE U.S. Customs Building on Battery Street, from which a full view of the bay could be had, two men stood at the window of an unassuming private office on the tenth floor. One of these men was young, keen-eyed, seemingly full of vitality in spite of the lines of weariness in his face. The other was a much older man, with coal-black hair and hard black eyes, a square, stubborn jaw that spoke of determination and the ability to finish whatever he started. It was in the hands of these two that the fate of America rested.

The younger man was known to his friends as Jimmy Christopher; in the records of the United States Intelligence he was only a number—Operator 5. The older man was known only as Z-7. Before the Purple Invasion, he had held in the fingers of his capable, stubby hands the threads of the entire United States Intelligence system, in all its ramifications throughout the world. He had been Operator 5's chief.

Now there was no longer an Intelligence Service. There was only a scattered remnant of the old department. But Z-7 had entered upon a new function—for he had been compelled to assume the titular leadership of the country's defense forces. It was Z-7 who had kept the invader from sweeping to the coast while Operator 5 was in South America gathering together the fleet of seaplanes which was now in the bay.

Those planes had returned only an hour ago, and Jimmy

Christopher had ordered them to be refueled, for they had exhausted the last drop of gasoline in the long flight.

They were both silent now as they stared out into the night. It was Z-7 who spoke, his face haggard with despair. "I tell you, Jimmy, it was unavoidable. They sent over a small army of planes, and they bombed all the oil fields, all the refineries. They knew you were coming with the planes, and they took measures to destroy all the available supply of oil in California. When we retreated from Oklahoma and Texas, we destroyed the wells there. Their supply is running low, and we would have been able to lick them easily—if I had only been able to prevent it—"

Jimmy Christopher put a soothing hand on the other's shoulder. "Don't blame yourself, Chief. There was nothing you could do about it. Rudolph was just a step ahead of us that time." He shrugged, forced a smile. "It's the fortunes of war, Chief. At least we have enough gas to put a few planes in the air. We can send serum to the towns that are infected with plague."

Z-7 nodded. "There are only about a dozen towns infected so far, and we've established a rigid quarantine around each. We hope to keep it from spreading. We—"

He stopped as a knock sounded at the door, and an orderly entered and saluted. "Baron Flexner, the emissary from the Central Empire, is growing impatient, sir," the orderly announced. "He demands that you see him at once."

Z-7 nodded somberly. "Show him in." He explained to Operator 5: "Baron Flexner is Rudolph's prime minister. He cabled a request for a conference, and I granted him a safe conduct. He flew in from Denver, and arrived while you were landing.

I asked him to wait, so we could both talk to him."

Jimmy Christopher shrugged. "It's easy to guess what he wants. Every few weeks Rudolph sends us a demand for unconditional surrender. But there are a couple of things I'd like to ask you before he comes in. First, is there any news of Nan?"

Nan Christopher, Operator 5's golden-haired, daring twin sister, had shared many of his adventures in the recent fighting in the East. She had gone to Canada a short while ago, and Jimmy had not received any news of her while he was in South America.

Z-7 nodded. "Nan contacted a group of Canadian ex-servicemen and former members of the Royal Canadian Mounted Police. She and a certain Sergeant MacTavish of the Mounties helped to smuggle them into the United States. With a small group she went to Rudolph's headquarters in Denver, to try to find whether the Central Empire chemists had discovered a serum for the plague. She reasoned that if they were spreading it among our cities they must have developed some new type of antitoxin by which they could readily immunize their own troops."

Jimmy frowned. "She shouldn't have gone there. It's too dangerous for a woman. She's so reckless, she may put her foot in it—"

He paused at sight of Z-7's grave expression. "I'm afraid she's already put her foot in it, Jimmy!

"What do you mean?"

For answer Z-7 reached for a thin sheet of onionskin paper on his desk, and handed it to Operator 5. "She smuggled out this message by carrier pigeon. It arrived only a few minutes ago."

Jimmy Christopher glanced at the message. It was in the old Z Code used by the United States Intelligence before the Purple Invasion, and Jimmy read it easily without recourse to a code book:

> Z-7 (ran the translation): I have contacted our old friend, Slips McGuire, and ten of us have found perfect hiding-place in the old Union Hotel, next door to the U.S. Mint where Emperor Rudolph has made his headquarters. We have perfect plan for discovering secret of laboratory in top floor of Mint Building, where it is said that cholera serum is being developed. Will report in detail later. Am sending this by carrier pigeon because radio unavailable. We have two pigeons, and in order to make sure you get this, am sending duplicate of this message by second pigeon an hour after the first. Tell Jimmy not to worry, will be home with the bacon.
>
> Nan.

Jimmy Christopher finished reading the message and looked up at Z-7. "Why do you say she's put her foot in it?

"That message, Jimmy," Z-7 told him slowly, "is in the old Z Code. Well, the Central Empire Military Police raided one of our branch offices in the East yesterday, and seized the Z Code Book. If they should spot that second pigeon and get the duplicate of this message, Nan's goose would be cooked out there in Denver, as well as that of the boys with her!"

Operator 5 whistled. "Let's hope the bird gets through. Now, what about this rumor of revolution in Mexico?"

Z-7 spread his hands helplessly. "Since the Purple Invasion, our espionage service is shattered. We don't know what's going on anywhere. All I have heard is that Rudolph plans to back General Arnaldo Barrenos in fomenting a revolution to overthrow the present government of Mexico, which is friendly to us yet."

"But we must stop that quick!" Operator 5 exclaimed. "Mexico is our only source of oil now. If Rudolph gains control of the Mexican oil fields, we're sunk—"

Just then the orderly entered again, stood at attention, and announced: "Baron Julian Flexner!"

The Baron was a tall man, thin almost to the point of emaciation, with a sallow countenance, and dry, bloodless lips. His small, shrewd eyes swept from Z-7 to Operator 5 in swift, keen appraisal. He waited until the orderly had left, then bowed from the waist, his lips twisting in a faint smile.

"I am honored, gentlemen," he said. His gaze fixed upon Jimmy Christopher. "I have the pleasure of addressing the—er—renowned person who is known as Operator 5?"

Jimmy nodded courteously. "I am Operator 5. This is my chief, the acting head of the United States Government, Z-7."

Flexner acknowledged the introduction. But he continued to address Jimmy. "You are a very clever man, Operator 5. All those seaplanes that I see in the bay—they constitute a powerful

8

armada, no?" He pursed his lips, and his eyes glinted sardonically. "It is too bad, is it not, that planes cannot be made to fly without petrol? How unfortunate—for your country—that my master, the Emperor Rudolph, destroyed your oil fields!"

Jimmy took a step forward, but controlled himself. "Did you come here to mock us, Baron Flexner, under the cloak of your safe conduct, or did you come on other business?"

Flexner suddenly dropped his pose of light banter. His eyes hardened, and his voice took on a brittle quality. "As you intimate, Operator 5, I come on business. I come with a proposal from my august master, His Imperial Highness, Rudolph I, Master of the Central Empire, Emperor of Europe, Asia, and the Americas!"

Jimmy smiled faintly. "Not yet of the Americas, my good Baron," he said softly. "There is yet a strip of our country unconquered. And we hope to widen the strip."

Flexner laughed harshly. "Operator 5, you are a fool. You cannot stand against the Central Empire. Shall I tell you why?" He stepped closer to them, wagged a finger from Z-7 to Jimmy Christopher. "For five years, the Central Empire prepared for this war of conquest. While your effete America prated of disarmament and world peace, we built great guns and fast planes and tanks and ships. We developed gases and methods of spreading bacteria. While you continued to dream idly in your false security, we conquered Europe, and then Asia. The Central Empire became the strongest military nation that the earth has ever seen, not barring the empire of Alexander or that of the Romans. We crossed the ocean and took you by storm. Your stubborn resistance is futile. We shall cross to the Pacific Ocean, and Emperor Rudolph will soon stand in this window, complete master of your country!"

HE PAUSED, and Jimmy wondered a moment at the strange fanaticism of this man. The lust for power shone in his eyes. He was a fit servant for the ruthless Rudolph I. "What do you propose?" he asked.

Flexner hurled his ultimatum. "Unconditional surrender! I come to convince you that further resistance is suicidal. My Emperor does not wish to destroy you altogether, unless he is compelled to do so. But if you resist, then we shall infect every city in the unconquered territory with the plague. You will die by the millions, like rats. We shall march across a land without a living soul. That is the ultimatum of my master. You have it in your hands to save the lives of millions of your countrymen. Speak now. What is your answer?"

He stopped, and a pregnant silence descended upon the room. But Baron Flexner was not through. In a lower voice he added, "There is one more condition which you must fulfill." His eyes were boring into those of Jimmy Christopher. "You, Operator 5, have three times escaped punishment at the hands of the Emperor. You have flouted him; you once made him to appear ridiculous before his troops; and once you almost captured him. Your life is forfeit. You must surrender yourself and return with me—otherwise no terms will be granted!"

For a long minute after Baron Flexner had finished, no word was spoken in the room. Jimmy Christopher and Z-7 exchanged glances, and a faint smile flickered in the Intelligence chief's

JIMMY CHRISTOPHER

eyes. Then he turned to Flexner, and said courteously: "Thank you for a pleasant ten minutes, Baron Flexner."

He pressed a button on his desk, and the orderly appeared at the door. "Kindly conduct the Baron to his plane," Z-7 instructed. "He is leaving at once."

Flexner gazed blankly from one to the other. "You—you refuse—?"

"We refuse, my dear Baron—unconditionally. Tell your master that he'll have to fight for every inch of ground he gets. You can't talk us out of it!"

Flexner's lips thinned to a tight line. "You think, perhaps, that you will be able to fight the plague with your serum? You will find you are mistaken. When you are convinced of that, send us a flag of truce. Within a few hours you will learn things—that you do not yet know!"

He bowed stiffly, and left the room.

Z-7 turned a troubled glance upon Operator 5. "What did he mean by that last, Jimmy? That devil has something up his sleeve...."

Jimmy Christopher turned and stared out of the window at the helpless seaplanes in the bay below. "You're sure it's cholera that's hit those cities?

"Yes. Asiatic cholera. It's a dreadful thing. They die like flies, some of them inside of an hour. But we've turned out a huge quantity of serum, and gotten it into every stricken city. If we can keep a victim alive for twenty-four hours, he has a ninety percent chance of recovering. With the amounts of serum we've sent them, they ought to be able to check the plague. I don't understand—"

Jimmy eyed his chief reflectively. "It might be a bluff," he mused. "Flexner's foxy. Perhaps he's banking on the heavy shock to morale that this plague has dealt. And then too, he may have overlooked the fact that Americans can take it. The peoples he's helped to dominate are being kicked around until they've reached the point where a plague tossed in would induce them to throw in the towel. It may be that he thinks our American men and women are of the same stuff."

But he spoke with doubt in his voice, as if he himself lacked confidence in his own suggestion.

Z-7 brightened. "By heaven, that may be it, Jimmy. It may be just a bluff, to cover up Rudolph's losses. That purple pirate must have gone out of his mind when he heard you'd gotten away with that forty million in gold, foxed Flexner in Brazil, and then sunk his navy at the Canal. Maybe this surrender demand is the result of a hasty conference that decided they'd have to make a bold play to cover up the loss of the navy.

"What's Rudolph doing with the Canal?" Jimmy asked.

Z-7 grinned. "You mean those bombed locks? He gave orders to have the Canal put into operating order in a hurry. But it was easier said than done. Those bombs you dropped tore the ribs off the mountains, and slides have been an almost daily occurrence since your visit.

"He'll clear the cut, though. His vanity will force him to do it. He was all puffed up when he captured the Canal and stood the world's shipping on its beam ends just to show he could do it. I don't see how he can gain anything of practical value, though.

"With nothing to shove through the Canal, no." Z-7 chuckled. "After you and the boys with those grand new planes of your design sent his wallowing warships to the bottom of the ocean, his little trick of trying a naval bombardment of our Pacific Coast lost its charm."

Jimmy Christopher nodded. "What's he doing with the dozen ships that got away?" he inquired.

"They're steaming back up the Atlantic Coast," Z-7 informed him. "They're not of much value, and even with the Canal cleared, he couldn't make much of an impression with them by moving them in to an attack on any of our Coast cities. Some of them will have to go into dry-dock after what you did to their decks and superstructure. In any case, I don't think Rudolph would move them into the Pacific, now that he knows we have airplanes.

"Airplanes," Jimmy grinned ruefully, "but no gasoline."

Z-7 shook his head. "That's tough. You did your part well. One thousand new planes, of your own design, capable of outflying and outfighting Rudolph's planes, and manned by as fine a lot of boys as a man could ask. If we only had gas!"

Jimmy sighed. "We could do a lot," he admitted. "But we can do a lot without the planes, and there's always the chance that we can make a quick raid on such supply bases as Rudolph will establish behind his lines. With a few planes of our own, using some of our scanty gas supply, we might swoop in and lift enough for considerable air operations."

Z-7's eyes glowed. "You've got an idea there, Operator 5. It's a peach! But—"his face fell "—we'll have to wait until Rudolph fills his own storage tanks.

"That may be soon," Jimmy said gravely.

"What do you mean?"

Jimmy locked his hands around one knee and rocked in his chair. "Rudolph's bound to send his henchmen scurrying around for oil—airplane gasoline or the raw material that he can develop into fuel for his planes. He's bound to begin dickering with oil-producing countries. Maybe Mexico." He shot a meaningful glance at Z-7.

Z-7 nodded. "We can rest easy there," he assured Operator 5. "The Mexican government is trying to keep well out of the way of Rudolph, but there's no friendship for Rudolph among the men in power in Mexico City.

"And Rudolph isn't fool enough to divert troops into Mexico at this stage of the game. He knows he'd weaken his forces on our front, and give us a chance to rally our forces to the point that he'd lose advantages he's gained in his drive from the Atlantic Coast to the Rocky Mountains.

"Yes, that's true," Jimmy agreed. "He'll dicker, though, first with the Mexican government, then with private interests. And he may succeed in obtaining a supply of oil. There's one thing to our advantage.

"What's that, Jimmy?

"If he decides he needs planes, and the fuel to keep them in the air, he may slacken his offensive. That'll give us time."

Z-7 nodded soberly, with a sympathetic glance at Jimmy.

"For one thing," he said slowly, "it'll give us time to try to reach Nan in Denver, and to—"

He was interrupted by the entrance of another orderly with a radio message. "It's from the mayor of San Diego, sir."

Z-7 read the message swiftly. His fist clenched. "By God!" he exclaimed. "The girl's crazy!" He swung on Operator 5. "Your friends Diane Elliot and Tim Donovan. Diane shouldn't do anything like this. We don't accept such sacrifices from women! And Tim's only a boy, after all. He shouldn't take such risks!"

Jimmy Christopher tautened with sudden anxiety. The name of Diane Elliot meant infinitely much to him. In the career he had chosen, there was no room for such an emotion as love. But if the time ever came when he could step out of the swirling current of adventure and peril, there was one person in the world whom he would not want to be without. That was Diane Elliot.

In his mind's eye there was a picture of her softly modeled face, of her keen, quick eyes shining with all the affection that she stored away in her breast for him. Meticulously, she had avoided every hint of sentiment in their personal relationship. She had shared many of his dangers, had gone with him along paths from which many would have turned back. And always by her keen wit and quick thinking, by her courage and audacity which at times almost matched his own, she had aided him materially in the perilous tasks he had undertaken.

Tim Donovan, though only a lad of fifteen, had attached himself to Operator 5 one night a couple of years ago, and had so demonstrated his native intelligence and wit that Operator 5 had grown to love the boy like a younger brother. Now, the both of them….

He took the radio message from Z-7's hands, and read it with growing anxiety:

Z-7
c/o SFC HEAD OFFICE
HAVE JUST RECEIVED WORD THAT CENTRAL

EMPIRE TROOPS ARE BESIEGING PHOENIX ARIZONA… TOWN ALMOST ENTIRELY DEMOL-ISHED BY DRUMFIRE… COLONEL GIVENS IN COMMAND THERE ASKING FOR HELP… HAVE NO ABLE MEN AT MY DISPOSAL… GROUP OF ONE THOUSAND WOMEN HAS BEEN ORGANIZED BY MISS DIANE ELLIOT… THEY HAVE LEFT WITH TEN TRUCKS OF SUPPLIES AMMUNITION AND MEDICAL STORES… SHE IS ACCOMPANIED BY YOUNG MAN TIM DONOVAN… THEY LEFT AT SEVEN PM… IF POSSIBLE PLEASE DISPATCH ANOTHER COLUMN TO SUPPORT THESE BRAVE WOMEN….

The message was signed by the Mayor of San Diego!

Z-7 WATCHED the play of emotion on Operator 5's face as he finished reading it. "What'll we do, Jimmy? It's a mad venture. They'll never be able to crash through to Phoenix. It's open country, and they'll be spotted in a jiffy. The enemy can drop a barrage on them and wipe them out in ten minutes. They've no artillery or anti-aircraft guns to defend themselves with!

"Look here, Z-7," Jimmy Christopher exclaimed abruptly. "You've called a conference of the division commanders for ten in the morning. You won't need me till then, and there's little we can do here. Let me take a plane and try to intercept that suicide column!"

Z-7 stroked his chin doubtfully. He walked over to the full-sized map on the wall, scrutinized it. "If they started at seven in

the evening, they must have passed El Centro long ago. They're probably around Gila Bend by this time. It's over six hundred miles, as the crow flies, to Phoenix. You'll probably get there about an hour too late. They'll either be in the town by then, or dead. Still, I'd like to see you try it, Jimmy."

Operator 5 was already pressing a button on Z-7's desk. To the orderly who appeared, he issued swift instructions. "I want a fast plane—one of those Boeings that we've just finished reconstructing. Have the machine guns tested, and the bomb racks filled. Phone the airport to have it ready in fifteen minutes. I'll be out there to take off at once!"

Z-7 came over to him, clasped his hand in a strong grip of understanding. "I'll take care of the seaplanes, Jimmy. Those that we can get gas for, I'll send out with serum. That's the most important thing right now—to get serum to the infected cities. And take care of yourself. I want you back here for the conference at ten." He pressed Operator 5's hand tightly. "God go with you, Jimmy!"

CHAPTER 1
THE YELLOW FLAG

T HE SUN rose over the heat-scorched lands of Arizona, and its first golden shafts of light slanting down upon the San Diego-Phoenix Highway revealed a sight seldom equaled in the annals of any nation—the sight of a thousand women marching to their deaths!

They were mostly young—girls in their late teens or early twenties, with here and there a more mature face or figure. Many wore the divided skirts and gaily colored blouses of the plains; others wore men's trousers and suede windbreakers, while still others were attired in the olive drab uniforms of the United States Army—uniforms formerly worn by fathers, husbands and brothers.

They plodded wearily eastward toward the city of Phoenix, and behind the advance contingent of marchers there rolled a score of heavy trucks, also driven by women. These trucks contained supplies—food, medicines, ammunition—which were sorely needed by the besieged American Defense Force within Phoenix.

From the east they could hear the dull, continuous rumble of the steady bombardment which the victorious invading troops of the conquering Central Empire had kept up all night.

Rudolph I, Emperor of the Central Empire, Master of Europe and Asia, had pushed his goose-stepping armies across America almost without opposition. The Purple Emperor, as he was known, had drenched the country in its own blood; and not until he had passed the Mississippi had the dazed defenders organized any effective resistance. Now, a desperate line of defense had hastily been flung down along the Colorado River and up through the Continental Divide, thence along the Yellowstone River to the Canadian border.

The superior armaments possessed by Rudolph enabled him to attack at a dozen points along this far-flung battle line, hammering away at weak spots with massed artillery. Our own great arms-manufacturing centers had been destroyed or captured in the early days of the invasion, so that we had only manpower to oppose to this array of steel; and the manpower must needs be strung out very thin along the two-thousand mile front.

Men were scarce. So the women of the country stepped into the breach. When word had reached San Diego that Phoenix was about to fall for lack of supplies, this column had been organized. And now, after a whole night's weary, toiling march, it was nearing its objective.

At its head rode a young woman in her early twenties, whose softly modeled face was fixed now in the grim lines of weariness. But her eyes were filled with a high resolve that overcame the deadly lassitude of her body. This young woman was Diane Elliot, formerly a star reporter for the Amalgamated Press. Now there was no longer an Amalgamated Press in the country, and Diane Elliot, like all these other women, was moving into battle to the aid of the nation's sorely pressed men. It was she who had organized this relief column, had kept it going through the night. Now, as her car topped a rise in the road, she said quickly: "Stop here, Tim!"

From this spot they were afforded a view of the long stretch of the Salt River Valley in which Phoenix lay. Behind them the column rumbled to a halt, and Diane Elliot's eyes swept over the scene of battle.

Far to the east, beyond the city, she could see the flashes of fire as the enemy guns thundered destruction. Phoenix itself lay in a mass of ruins. White clouds of dust arose from it as shell after shell burst there. Using a pair of binoculars, Diane focused them on a spot in the center of town, where she had glimpsed a suspicion of life. For a long time she held the glasses glued to her eyes, while the column behind shifted uneasily.

The driver of the car, whom she had addressed as Tim, was the only person of the male sex in that contingent. He was a freckle-faced, pug-nosed lad of not more than fifteen, yet he drove the car with the skill and steadiness of a much older man.

This lad was Tim Donovan, a boy who had distinguished himself in the defense of the country in notable manner.*

* AUTHOR'S NOTE: Readers of previous novels in this magazine will already have recognized both Diane Elliot and Tim Donovan as two members of

Now, Diane Elliot's face seemed to pale as she studied the scene of battle. Abruptly, she handed the glasses to the freckled-faced lad at the wheel, said tensely: "Tell me what you see there, Tim. I—I hope—I'm mistaken!"

Many of the women grouped around the car as Tim Donovan took the glasses from her, threw her a curious glance, then focused them on the valley.

"Well?" Diane demanded. "What do you see?"

AFTER A moment, Tim spoke. "It looks like the defenders are barricaded in the center of the town, Di. They've torn up the streets, and it looks like they've dug trenches across the city. I can spot several machine-gun nests. They're getting ready for close-in fighting when the enemy stops the bombardment and advances. Rudolph's troops are less than a mile from the town. What I can't understand is why they haven't encircled the city. They could have done it, easy—"

that small but determined band which acknowledged Operator 5 as their leader. Each one of that small band has been chosen by Operator 5 for his or her innate courage, resourcefulness and determination. And those qualities had been amply tested in the past—tested under conditions which would have spelled death for themselves and destruction for the country, had it not been for the quick thinking, the instantaneous resourcefulness, and the loyal courage of this little band. And they asked nothing better than to be permitted to stake their lives in the service of their country—as they were doing now.

He stopped as Diane gripped his arm. "And can you understand why Colonel Smith and the defenders haven't retreated? They could have pulled out of there during the night, and escaped. As it is, their position is hopeless."

Tim Donovan frowned, swept the field with the glasses. "It's funny, Di. It looks like the Central Empire overlooked a bet when they didn't surround the town—

"Look carefully, Tim," Diane broke in. "Look over there, to the left of the City Hall ruins, over by the railroad station. That's where the defenders seem to be grouped thickest. What—do you see there?"

Tim obeyed, and suddenly, as his glasses became fixed on a certain object, he gulped, pressed them harder to his eyes, as if the action might aid him to verify what he saw. Abruptly, he lowered the binoculars, and his face was suddenly drained of color, as Diane Elliot's had been a moment ago.

"Di! That—that's a—*yellow flag* they're flying. A quarantine flag! They've got the plague there!"

Diane nodded, catching a sob in her throat. "That—that's why the enemy isn't advancing to capture the town. They—intend to shell it into the ground!"

She took the glasses from the boy, looked through them herself, once more. "Did you see those men lying prone on the ground, Tim? I thought at first they were sniping at the enemy. They aren't. They're dying—dying of cholera!"

The group of women who had gathered about the car drew closer. Each of these women wore a green band about her left arm, to signify that she was a junior officer in command of a section of the column. They had heard what Diane said, and now their eyes were filled with panic. One of them, a tall, fair-haired girl of twenty-two, said in hushed voice: "Miss Elliot! What will we do now? If we go in there, we'll get the plague—"

Diane stopped her. "Look here, Clara, we knew when we started out that there was a possibility of this. We knew that the plague had hit a dozen cities on the west coast, and they're all quarantined. Operator 5 is working hard to discover an antitoxin that can be produced in large quantities. In the meantime we have some serum here with us among these supplies. Phoenix is doomed unless we get in there.... What are we going to do about it?"

Clara Blaine hesitated. The other women about her began to whisper among themselves in awed voices. These girls and women had seen husbands and brothers shot down in battle within recent months, had willingly endured untold privations and hardship at home in order that there might be sufficient supplies for the American Defense Force; they were even willing to face death themselves—but the prospect of becoming infected with the dreadful Asiatic cholera was one that caused even the bravest among them to grow pale.

It was only within the last few days that the Purple Emperor had begun to use the dreadful plague bacteria in his campaign to subjugate the balance of the United States. Reports had come from a dozen widespread points—from Salt Lake City, from Helena, Montana, from Spokane and from Seattle—of the sudden spread of the dreadful plague. Enemy airplanes had dropped a new type of bomb, containing millions of bacilli of the type *cholera*. Within twenty-four hours hundreds of inhabitants of those cities had been stricken, and the frightful specter of the loathsome disease was stalking unchecked through the streets. It was three days now since the first reports had come through, and thousands of men, women and children had already died, writhing out their last hours in appalling agony. Quarantines had been established about those cities and no person was permitted to enter or leave on pain of immediate execution.

Thus far, the enemy's bacteriological warfare had been confined to a few key spots well behind the line of battle—for obvious reasons.* Now, however, Diane and her column encoun-

---

* AUTHOR'S NOTE: It is, of course, a first principle of modern warfare to weaken or cripple the enemy at the source of his supplies. At the outset of the Purple Invasion, the Central Empire had enjoyed a preponderance of war materials, including airplanes, and had thus been enabled to bomb and destroy our great centers of armament manufacture. Thus from the very beginning, we were reduced to a species of guerrilla warfare, and those who have read the preceding chronicles of this war will recall how well Operator 5 organized this guerrilla fighting. But as the months passed on and the resistance of the Americans, instead of weakening, grew ever more stubborn, the Emperor Rudolph turned at last to the only means he could conceive of for breaking the morale of our defenders—bacteria. Although bacteriological warfare has been specifically banned under the Articles of War promulgated at the Hague Convention, the Purple Emperor felt no compulsion to obey them—for the simple reason that there no longer existed

tered it face-to-face at the battle front, and the prospect quite evidently did not appeal to Clara Blaine and the other women. Somehow, word had spread down the balance of the column of the situation in Phoenix, and a wave of panic rolled back among the weary marchers. Diane Elliot realized that it would be too much to ask them to enter the city and expose themselves to hideous death. With abrupt decision, she arose in the car and issued swift orders.

"THERE ARE two trucks in this column containing medical supplies. I want them driven up here to the head of the column!" she commanded.

She waited while the order was transmitted to the drivers, and in a moment the two canvas-covered trucks pulled up in the road alongside her car. Clara Blaine and the other women looked on questioningly.

"I am going to turn the column over to you, Clara," she went on.

The tall, flaxen-haired Clara Blaine stepped forward impulsively. "Miss Elliot—what—are you going to do?"

such a thing as "Rules of International Warfare." The Central Empire had marched victoriously over all of Europe and a good part of Asia. The Hague itself was swallowed up in the Purple Empire; and if Rudolph had his way in America, there would soon be no flag anywhere but the crossed broadswords and the severed head which was the insignia under which Rudolph I planned to conquer the world.

Diane's lips tightened. "I am going to drive one of those trucks into Phoenix. I want one volunteer to drive the other." There was a slight tinge of scorn in her voice. "Maybe there's just one of you who's willing to take a chance in order to get these supplies in there. I hope that isn't asking too much!"

The women wavered. Many of them were on the point of volunteering. But just then a voice piped up from the car. "Me, Di!"

It was Tim Donovan. He jumped from the car, pushed up alongside her. "I'm the guy, Di."

Now the women crowded around them. They had needed only that little spur to dissipate their wavering indecision. Dozens of voices were raised eagerly: "I'll go, Miss Elliot! Let me drive! And me!"

Diane laughingly waved them aside. "I'm taking Tim Donovan. He was the first to volunteer, so he's entitled to the chance."

With a whoop Tim climbed into the leading truck, bowed to the girl at the wheel and said: "Excuse me miss, you're fired!"

The girl descended, leaving Tim in full possession. In the meantime Diane had been issuing swift orders to Clara Blaine. "You'll take the column back to Wickenburg and hold it there. It would be impossible for all of us to get into Phoenix anyway. The enemy would spot us in a minute, and they could blow us off the road."

But Clara Blaine objected. "I won't do it, Miss Elliot. I'm sorry I was such a coward. We won't let you and Tim Donovan go in there alone. We'll all go!"

From the group about them came a chorus of enthusiastic

support. "Clara's right. What's the difference if it's cholera or shrapnel? You can only die once anyway!"

Diane shook her head. "I'm sorry, girls, but only Tim and I are going. I feel bad enough about exposing Tim to the plague, without bringing you all into it as well—"

She broke off as Tim's excited voice interrupted: *"Take cover, everybody!* They've spotted us!"

His voice was drowned by the terrific whining screech of a heavy shell. Instinctively the group about Diane threw themselves to the ground, and the rest of the column scattered into the fields on both sides of the road. The earth trembled under the concussion, and a great geyser of dirt, concrete, steel and wood rose up in the air as the high-powered projectile struck in a direct hit on one of the ammunition trucks at the rear of the column.

Diane had flung herself to the ground alongside Jimmy's truck, and she raised her eyes to the sky, following his pointing finger. "There's the guy that gave them the range!" He was pointing to an enemy observation plane that was circling high overhead. Under its wings they could distinctly see the scarlet emblem, of the crossed broadswords and the severed head, which was the insignia of the Central Empire.

Hardly had Tim spoken before a second and a third shell screamed overhead. Instinctively, Tim and Diane ducked, but the shell struck far behind them on the road, this time crashing into two more trucks. Now the enemy barrage began coming over in deadly earnest. Without giving them a breathing spell, projectile after projectile crashed into the column of trucks.

HIS
IMPERIAL
MAJESTY
RUDOLPH I
EMPEROR of
AMERICA

J. FLEMING GOULD
SCULPTOR

A dense gray haze of smoke and dust spread over the road, extending to the fields on either side, as more and more of the enemy artillery came into play. Great pits were gouged into the fields and into the road, and dozens of  the fleeing women died. There was no safety in those fields, and there was no way of escape to the rear, for the deadly barrage was building a curtain of fire behind them. At the same time additional shells were coming over at shorter range, and Tim and Diane could see the explosions creeping up the road toward the two trucks where they had taken shelter. Tim Donovan jumped down from the truck and crouched beside Diane. "We better get out of here, Di," he shouted in her ear. "They'll reach us any second now."

Diane was about to reply when she suddenly shuddered, shrank with dread-filled eyes from a gruesome object which thudded into the road alongside the truck. It was a woman's headless body. "That blouse!" she cried. "That—that's Clara Blaine!"

Tim Donovan's youthful face was twisted in revulsion. He sprang up, braving the hail of fire, and shook his little fist in the direction of the invisible artillery which was hurling death at them from miles away. "Damn you!" he shouted hoarsely. "Can't you see these are women?" Diane reached up frantically and dragged him down beside her. "Tim, Tim. That doesn't do any good!"

"All right," he growled. "Come on, Di, let's get out of here!"

"How, Tim?"

"There's only one way, Di—that's forward. We'll each take a truck and make a dash for it!"

Diane's eyes flashed. "Okay! Come on!"

She leaped up, and clambered into the second truck. Tim got into the cab of the first truck. The shells were coming close now, moving inexorably up toward the head of the column. All that portion of the road along which the column had been halted was now nothing but a jagged crevasse of twisted metal and tortured flesh.

Diane leaned out of the truck and waved toward the figures of the women who had taken cover in the fields. She watched breathlessly while they began to run toward the trucks singly and in small groups of twos and threes. Soon all the survivors had clambered into the tonneaus of the two trucks. Of all that column who had marched the whole night, not more than fifty had survived the five-minute bombardment. Diane signaled to Tim, and the two trucks set off down the road, heading straight for the besieged city of Phoenix.

CHAPTER 2
CITY OF DOOM

TIM DONOVAN, in the leading truck, drove with his fists gripping the wheel tightly, and with his foot jamming the accelerator down into the floorboards. Three girls who had raced to the truck from the field were crowded into the cab beside him. They sat tense, with white, shocked faces. They had just gone through an experience which was enough to deaden the nerves of a strong man. They had not yet recovered from the sight of the torn bodies of their friends in that field alongside the road. One of them, a slender, dark-haired girl of about nineteen, still gripped a submachine gun in her two thin hands. She had held on to it all through the bombardment, and had run with it to the truck, too dazed to drop it.

Tim stared straight ahead, down the long ribbon of road which descended into Phoenix. He could see that the bombardment of the city had ceased while the enemy artillery had raised its sights to annihilate the column. There was still a mile and a half between them and the city. He wondered if they would be able to make it. The truck was gathering speed on the downgrade, but he did not take his foot from the gas, and they went hurtling ahead like a thunderbolt. Diane's truck followed, less than fifty feet behind.

Suddenly, above the whir of his motor, Tim heard another sound—the ominous buzzing drone of an airplane motor!

He snatched his eyes from the road ahead, and risked a glance upward. The observation plane which had directed the artillery fire from a distance was zooming down directly at them!

The girl with the submachine gun exclaimed: "Will he—shoot at us?"

Tim laughed harshly. "Why not, sister? See those guns mounted on his wings? Why shouldn't he use them?

32

"B-because t-these are medical supply trucks. They both have red crosses on the tops."

Even as she spoke, the plane came down at a low dive. The deafening roar of its engines drowned out the sounds of the truck's motor. The plane loomed huge above them and slightly to the left, and red flame belched from the two machine guns mounted on its wings! Tracer bullets whined into the tonneau of the truck, ripping through the canvas covering. There was just the single spurt and then the plane zoomed past, its undercarriage barely missing the top of the truck. Tim's lips tightened, and his knuckles grew white on the steering wheel. He kept his foot hard down on the accelerator. From the tonneau behind came the moan of a woman. The girl with the submachine gun twisted around and looked inside. "Oh God!" she exclaimed in a low voice. "Someone's hit in there!"

Tim said bitterly: "Well, sister, that's how much good your red cross does." He was suddenly conscious that the deafening sound of the artillery fire had ceased. A great silence had abruptly descended upon the plain, a silence which was more ominous than the drumfire of the bombardment. It was as if the enemy were taking time out to watch the airplane play with the two trucks. The aviator had looped, gotten altitude, and was coming down again in a fast power dive, with both machine guns spouting hot streams of lead at Tim's truck. Again, Tim raced ahead with taut muscles while the enemy crate leveled out and raked them with a hail of slugs. He was concentrating on the first truck, and as yet Diane's car, behind, was unscathed.

This time the stream of lead from the plane's port gun cut

in at an angle through the cab and shattered the windshield. It missed Tim and the girl with the machine gun who sat beside him, but he could distinctly hear the dull thud of lead against flesh as the bodies of the two girls next to her were riddled. The one on the end uttered a shrill scream and pitched sideways out of the cab to roll into the ditch beside the road, and lie there in a pitiful, grotesquely huddled heap. The other girl slumped from her seat to the floor of the cab, and crimson blood spurted from a bullet hole in her left breast.

The thin girl with the machine gun covered her eyes and shrank back against Tim, crowding against his elbow. She began to sob hysterically. The plane zoomed, seeking altitude for another dive. Tim bit his lip in helpless rage. From the covered part of the truck there came more moans and cries of agony. Others had been hit in that second fusillade from the plane. Tim said grimly to the girl beside him: "What's your name, sister?"

Between sobs she stuttered: "M-Marie J-Joyce.

"All right, Marie, quit the hysterics. This is war. Can you drive a car?"

She gulped, choked back a sob, and brushed the back of her hand across her eyes. Then she raised her head bravely. "Yes. I can drive a car."

"Okay, Marie. When I pull myself up, slide in under me and grab the wheel."

She obeyed. Now there was no hesitancy about her actions. For an instant the truck slowed when Tim took his foot from the accelerator, but almost immediately it regained its speed as Marie Joyce pressed her foot down upon it once more. Her slim hands held the heavy wheel firm, and she kept her eyes glued to the road. This opportunity to do something concrete had driven the hysteria from her. "What are you going to do?" she asked Tim breathlessly.

"Just watch," he told her grimly. "And no matter what happens, you keep your foot glued to the floorboard. There's less than a mile to go now. If we can only get rid of that plane, we'll have a chance to make it!"

AHEAD OF them the battered ruins of the city of Phoenix were plainly visible now. The yellow quarantine flag could be seen without binoculars. And as the truck raced on at seventy miles an hour, the city seemed to be rushing up to meet them. But overhead, the black plane with the scarlet emblem of the crossed broadswords and the severed head was thundering down at them once more. Already its twin machine guns were spitting lead and flame.

For a moment, Marie Joyce's startled eyes were fixed on that roaring monster of destruction, swooping down upon them; and the thought raced through her mind that it might be better to die under those spouting guns than to reach the city, where a more hideous form of death waited for them in the form of the virulent cholera.

But quickly she thrust the thought from her as she saw that Tim Donovan had snatched up her machine gun, slung it over his back by the strap. He stepped up on the seat, moving carefully to avoid the slumped body of the dead girl on the floor, and then he reached up, seized the top of the cab, and hoisted himself outside, onto the roof. The hot wind tore at him, tried to pry him loose from the precarious perch on the top, and to fling him out onto the road. But he clung grimly with one hand, while he unslung the machine gun with the other.

Now the plane was almost upon them, and he could see the goggled, helmeted face of the Central Empire aviator peering down at him, while the two machine guns stuttered in staccato accompaniment to the drone of the powerful engines. Lead

Frantically the pilot crossed his controls, seeing in that split
second that he was flying straight into the jaws of death.

spattered the cab top, and bullets ricocheted all about him. Tim faced the sudden hail of lead, raised the machine gun to his shoulder, and sighted well ahead of the whizzing plane. Grimly he yanked at the trip, and the submachine gun began to kick against his shoulder, bucking with each second-fast round of shots. A thin stream of lead whined upward from his muzzle in the path of the oncoming plane. The aviator, suddenly sensing his peril, tried to veer suddenly, and the wind screamed in his struts as he banked sharply.

Tim's fusillade cut into the right wing of the plane, sewing a black line of holes across the scarlet emblem painted on it. Frantically the pilot crossed his controls, seeing in that split second that he was flying straight into the jaws of death; but the sudden strain of that quick banking turn, plus the line of slugs, weakened the wing, and it buckled, the weight of the machine gun mounted upon it tearing it down. The plane twisted on its side, there was a rending screech of ripping metal, and Tim had one single glance of the aviator's startled face as the truck sped by underneath. Then, the plane was left behind, and Tim twisted to watch it. He saw it stagger into a drunken chandelle, pause a moment in midair, then dive, nose first, into the field.

Flames spewed from it as it telescoped into the ground. In a moment it was only a twisted mass of burning wreckage.

Tim's youthful face was set in hard lines. "That pays off in part for those dead girls!" he muttered.

It was a tribute to Marie Joyce's steadiness that the truck did not slow down at all. Tim clambered down, threw her a quick smile, and crouched beside her.

"You got him!" she exclaimed, almost unbelievingly.

"Yeah. Now, keep going. Maybe we can make it!"

He leaned out of the cab, looked behind, and saw that Diane's truck was following close behind them. He nodded in satisfaction, and looked forward.

They were roaring down the slope of the road, and were already in the outlying section of Phoenix. Here there were widely spaced residences, which had not been damaged by the bombardment. But there was no sign of life. They were all deserted, their owners either having fled or joined the defenders in the center of town.

The truck flashed along until the road became a street. Straight ahead they could see the barricades erected by the defenders, could see the figures of men waving to them in wild acclaim. Marie Joyce took her foot from the accelerator, slowed up. They jolted over broken-up streets, pitted by shellfire, and denuded of bricks which had been torn up for the barricades.

In front of City Hall she braked to a stop, and Diane's truck halted immediately behind them. They were at once surrounded by the frenziedly joyous defenders. Joyce and Tim descended from the truck, and Diane came running over to them. She threw her arms around Tim, hugged him.

"That was grand, Tim! I saw you on top of the truck!"

A TALL man pushed through the crowd to their side. He wore the uniform of a colonel of infantry, and the tired lines that were etched under his eyes spoke of the sleepless nights he had spent. "I am Colonel Givens," he told them, "commanding the defenders of Phoenix. We watched you come in. It was splendid!" His voice suddenly dropped, assuming an anxious, eager tone. "Tell me—have you got any—cholera serum?"

Diane nodded. "There's some in each truck.

"Thank God!" he exclaimed. He pointed across the square, to where rows of men and women lay on the ground behind a crude breastworks. Now, at closer view, Diane and Tim could see the mottled expressions on their faces, could see how they writhed in agony.

"We've got two hundred cholera cases," Colonel Givens went on. "We had more than two thousand. The others have died—mercifully. We've got to treat them here, under the barricades, since the hospital was blown up. Perhaps we can save some of them, prevent it from spreading—now that we have the serum."

He motioned to one of the many doctors who were moving about among the stricken ones, called out joyfully: "Doctor Styles! There's serum in these trucks! Come and get it!"

"And stretchers for our wounded," Diane added. "Several of the girls in this first truck were hit by the plane." She lowered her eyes, gulped. "We, too, have had some casualties, Colonel. There—were a thousand of us only a few minutes ago. Now there are less than fifty!"

Colonel Givens said in a hushed voice: "That was a brave thing to do. But you shouldn't have come. We would never have sent an appeal for help if we had known that women would march to our aid. We are doomed here, anyway. Even if we could escape, we would not avail ourselves of the chance; for every one of us probably carries the cholera. We'd spread it everywhere behind the lines!"

Tim Donovan had already left them, and had wandered ahead, up to where the barricades had been erected. They consisted of bricks and huge blocks of cement from shattered buildings, bolstered up with sacks of wet earth. The entire breastworks had been built up to a height of three feet, and stretched across the entire square and into the adjacent streets.

Behind this hasty barricade, men and women crouched with rifles and machine guns. In the ruins of every building on the square, Tim saw other machine-gun nests. There were perhaps five or six hundred defenders behind the barricades, and they all bore hopeless, weary expressions. There was, indeed, little hope for them. If the enemy shells did not finally blast them out of their entrenchments, they had only to look forward to a hideous death from cholera.

Colonel Givens led Diane and the other women from the trucks over to the square, and introduced them to his junior officers. Marie Joyce uttered a glad cry, and ran impulsively into the arms of a young man in the uniform of a lieutenant of engineers who was among the colonel's aides.

"Frank!" she cried. The young lieutenant gazed at her with horrified glance.

"Marie! God, why did you come? There's cholera here!" He clasped her in his arms, pressed her tight, and buried his head in her dark hair.

Colonel Givens told Diane: "That's Lieutenant Frank Satterlee. Who's the girl?"

"She's Marie Joyce," Tim broke in. "A swell kid. She drove the truck in. Satterlee must be her boyfriend."

Diane nodded. "They're engaged. That's why Marie wanted to come with the column. She begged me to take her along. Now they're united—but God knows for how long!"

Colonel Givens was not listening to her. He was gazing eastward, past the ruins of the city, toward where a thin scar in the earth indicated the trenches of the enemy line. The gray-clad, steel-helmeted troops were showing themselves carelessly, secure in the knowledge that the town's defenders had no guns capable of reaching them. A squadron of tanks was lined up slightly to the north, with the long snouts of their guns poking upward. But they were not firing. The bombardment had ceased.

"I wonder," the colonel said uneasily, "why they've quit the drumfire. They've been shelling us steadily all night. Now that you're here, they suddenly let up. What's back of it?"

Diane shrugged, was about to speak, when they were attracted by a shout. They turned to see Doctor Styles running toward them from the sick-line. He was a small, stout man in his late forties, bald-headed, but with a heavy black moustache. He came up to them panting, waving a vial which he held in one hand. In his other was a hypodermic syringe. He gasped out: "Colonel Givens! This serum is no good! God! It's useless!"

Givens seized his arm. "What do you mean, man? What are you saying?" He glanced inquiringly at Diane Elliot.

Diane exclaimed: "It's fresh serum, doctor! We waited until

the last minute, until the base hospital at San Diego got it ready for us."

"Yes, yes, I know, Miss Elliot. But it's not the serum that's at fault. I've been unable to test the bacillus of the plague until I got some of it. I've just completed a test. And I find something terrible." He paused a moment, then went on slowly: *"This is a new kind of cholera bacillus.* Those fiends must have discovered it in Asia. We can neither prevent nor cure this plague with the serum we now have!"

Colonel Givens let a deep sigh escape him. "You mean, Doctor, that there is no hope for us—even with the serum?"

"That is what I mean—God help us!"

CHAPTER 3
DEATH THE BESIEGER

THE BLARE of a bugle drew the attention of Diane, Tim and Colonel Givens from Dr. Styles' shocking news. One of the enemy tanks was rolling across the field toward the town. But it was not thundering death. Its turret was open, and a Central Empire trooper with a white flag in his hand stood beside the scarlet flag of the Purple Empire. Behind the trooper they could see a staff officer.

Colonel Givens exclaimed incredulously: "A white flag! What can they have to say to us?"

Tim Donovan made a wry face. "Don't trust those buzzards, Colonel," he said. "They're probably up to some deviltry."

The tank rumbled to a halt a hundred feet from the barricade.

The Central Empire staff officer cupped his hands and called out in English: "Let me talk to your commander!"

Colonel Givens frowned puzzledly, shrugged and said to Diane: "I don't know why they should come with a white flag. All they have to do is resume their bombardment and they could blot us off the earth in a few more hours. However, I'll talk to him." He moved forward, and climbed across the barricade amid a dead silence from his own men. Young Lieutenant Satterlee and another junior officer followed the colonel, flanking him on either side. When Givens had come within twenty feet of the tank the Central Empire staff officer called out hastily: "Come no further. That is close enough."

Givens threw up a questioning glance. "But you wished to talk to me—"

"We can talk as we are now," the officer grinned. "I have no wish to come closer to one who carries the cholera!"

Colonel Givens nodded in dignified manner. "So be it. What have you to say?"

"I," said the man on the tank, "am Major Stepan Horty, of the Headquarters Staff of Marshal Kremer commanding the Imperial Army of His Majesty Rudolph I. Marshal Kremer sends me with a message."

The American commander bowed. "I am Colonel Givens, commanding the Ninth Volunteer Regiment, defending this sector. You may deliver your message to me."

"It is this. You and those under your command in this city are completely at our mercy. We have just wiped out the relief column which was bringing you supplies. We could lay down a

44

curtain of drumfire that would annihilate every living being in the city of Phoenix. But Marshal Kremer is merciful and generous. He instructs me to tell you that he spares your lives. He will give you one hour to evacuate the city. You may take your sick and wounded with you, and you will not be molested. But after one hour we will occupy the city, and anyone found here will be shown no mercy!"

"Thank you, Major Horty," said Colonel Givens.

"You accept the terms, then?"

"I must return to the barricades, and consult with my junior officers."

"Very well. But we must have your answer before the hour has expired. If you accept, run up a white flag as a signal."

While Colonel Givens and the American defenders watched silently, the tank clumsily maneuvered about and returned toward the enemy trenches. Colonel Givens came back wearily across the barricade. Many of the defenders clustered about him, all talking excitedly and speculating on the reasons for Marshal Kremer's sudden clemency.

Colonel Givens drew Diane, Tim and Lieutenant Satterlee to one side. "What do you think?" he asked. "Can it be a trap of some sort?"

"In what way can it be a trap?" Lieutenant Satterlee demanded. "Marshal Kremer—"

"Is a shrewd old fox!" Diane finished for him, glancing at lovely young Marie Joyce, who had moved over to Satterlee's side and had unobtrusively taken his hand.

Colonel Givens frowned. "Old fox? I do not understand. He

TIM
DONOVAN

is a shrewd enough general. It is he who is responsible for most of Rudolph's military successes. But what trick can he have in mind—"

"I'll tell you, sir!" Tim Donovan broke in excitedly. "I think I know why Kremer is willing to let us walk out of here!"

BY THIS time many of the men and women defenders had

gathered about the small group. They all looked curiously at this youngster, who presumed to talk with such assurance.

Colonel Givens said impatiently: "Well, if you have any ideas, young man, let's have them quickly. We haven't much time—"

"You see, sir," Tim explained earnestly, "Kremer can't be actuated by any merciful motives. A merciful man would never have dropped cholera germs in the city in the first place. Now, every man and woman in Phoenix is infected with the plague. Don't you see that by allowing us to leave the city, he expects us to seek refuge among the American Defense Forces. He expects us to spread the cholera infection throughout the rest of the country. That's his motive in sparing us!"

There were startled murmurs from those who had gathered around them. Up to this moment all these people had been too busy fighting, too busy waiting for death from the shrieking, rending shrapnel, to give much thought to the fear of the plague. Now the dreadful realization struck them with full force—the realization that they were pariahs among men. There was no road to safety or happiness for them. Wherever they went among their friends and among those they loved, they would bring the danger of the hideous plague. Now, Tim Donovan had stated their position in a few succinct words.

Colonel Givens uttered a low oath, and his suddenly haggard face swept over the countenances of those who were crowded about them. "God!" he muttered, "the lad is right. We can't accept Kremer's mock mercy. To save our lives would be to imperil the rest of the country!"

An old man pushed through the crowd to face the colonel.

This man's hair was pure white, and though the weight of years rested upon him, he carried himself erect. The others made way for him respectfully. He wore a tattered gray uniform, the insignia upon the collar of which was so tarnished and worn that it was unrecognizable. He carried upon his shoulder an old musket of a type long since discarded by the United States Army. And for all his age he bore himself with dignified, military erectness.

Colonel Givens looked down at him kindly. "What is it, Captain Allen? Have you a suggestion?"

The old man nodded. "I have, Colonel. This uniform that you see on me, and this musket here, saw service before you were born. There is no one of you young folks here now, who recognizes this uniform."

"I do," Diane Elliot said quickly, with a strange warmth in her glance. "My grandfather wore such a uniform. It is the uniform of the Second South Carolina Volunteers. They fought at Manassas—in General Johnston's Confederate Army."

The old man looked at her keenly, studying her features. "Aye, girl, my memory is still good. I see the resemblance. You've inherited your grandfather's features. You'll be Major Harry Elliot's granddaughter!"

Diane nodded. "That's right. And you're Captain Allen. I remember granddad used to tell stories of how you captured a Yankee standard at Manassas."

Old Captain Allen chuckled. "Aye, so I did. The Yankees called it Bull Run. But by whatever name they call it, we beat them that day!" Abruptly he swung on Givens. "Colonel!" he barked. "You're faced with this situation—remain here, and be

48

blown to hell; evacuate the city and spread the cholera throughout the land. Am I right?"

"That's true," Givens said brokenly. "We haven't much choice—"

"Oh yes, we have! I am an old man, and I have lived too long already. I don't know how you young'uns feel, but I am ready to die. Don't you remember that line that the poet once wrote—" His voice took on a strange note of power as he declaimed—

> " 'To every man upon this earth
> Death cometh soon or late.
> And how can man die better
> Than facing fearful odds,
> For the ashes of his fathers,
> And the temples of his Gods!' "

Allen turned slowly, his old eyes darting from face to face. "Every one of us here must die. Life is a little thing to give for liberty. And if we must die, let's do it with a bang. Let's not wait here to be blasted by artillery fire. And let's not go back to spread disease among our friends. *Let's counter-attack.* Let's charge the enemy the way we used to do in the good old days. *Let's carry these cholera germs across the lines!* We'll die—every last one of us. But it will be a glorious way to die!"

A wave of fanatical enthusiasm seemed to sweep over the group of people who had heard the old man's impassioned words. Cries began to go up from all around them: "Let's attack! Let's attack!"

Tim Donovan jumped in and shook the old man's hand.

"You've got the right idea, grandpop. That was some speech you handed out!"

Captain Allen held Tim's hand, looking at him compassion-ately. He said, suddenly low-voiced: "You're very young, my boy—too young to die. Why, you're only a kid."

Tim's eyes were fearless. "I've had it coming for a long time, grandpop. I've got the cholera now, I suppose, the same as you and everybody else here. So I must die with you. I guess—" the boy's voice was suddenly somber and his eyes thoughtful—"I've always had a sneaking fear of death. But that poem spoke—seemed to take all the sting out of dying!"

While Tim was talking to old Captain Allen, a feverish, enthusiastic activity had taken possession of the defenders of the barricades. Colonel Givens, with Diane at his side, was issu-ing curt, swift orders to his aides. Extra rounds of ammunition, together with bayonets for those who had rifles, were being passed out. Men were scouring the nearby ruins for sharp imple-ments of any kind. For this would be an undertaking entailing the use of cold steel. Everyone there was determined to sell his life as dearly as possible when he reached the enemy trenches—and in the very act of dying to conquer—by spreading the dread-ful plague infection they carried. Even those lying in agony in the sick-line arose against the protests of Dr. Styles and found themselves arms of some kind. They welcomed this chance at a hero's death.

COLONEL GIVENS had become a dynamo of energy. His military ability showed itself in the dispositions which he made for the sortie. "We'll attack in three waves," he said. "Number one group will be composed of thirty men, each carrying one of our submachine guns. You, Wilstach—" nodding to one of his aides—"will take charge of the machinegun contingent. You are not to use the guns, but to carry them as far toward the enemy's line as you can before you're shot down. That means that you will be the first to die. But the second wave will be able to pick up those guns where you leave them, and carry on."

Wilstach, a dour-faced Scotch-American, shrugged. "Might as well go first as last," he said indifferently. His face was a mottled gray, and his forehead was beaded with sweat. There was fever in his eyes and he constantly held a hand pressed tight against his stomach, where pains seemed to grip him continuously. The plague had hit him only a little while before, but he was carrying on just the same.

Givens next turned to a tall, redheaded captain of infantry. "You, Grogan, will take the second wave. You'll have two hundred men. At the signal, you go over the top, pick up the machine guns, and carry on the charge. Satterly, you'll come with me with the third wave. It'll be our job to clean out the enemy trench. We've got to act in this thing as if we anticipated success. Of course, the majority of us will be mowed down before we get anywhere hear the trench. But those of us who survive must carry the fight to the enemy."

Diane asked him timidly: "What about the women, Colonel? There are about fifty of us who came with the column, and I see you have almost another hundred here."

"You, Miss Elliot, will take command of the women. You will cover the attack with rifles from behind the barricades. That is the best I can do for you. I have not the courage to order you to attack—"

Diane nodded. "We'll take care of that, Colonel. We—"

She stopped as the high, droning buzz of an airplane came to their ears from the northwest. Looking tensely in that direction, they saw a swift biplane winging directly toward them, with the insignia of the United States Air Force on the fuselage. Apparently the Central Empire troops had sighted it at the same time, for a couple of anti-aircraft guns opened up on it from behind the enemy lines, and bursts of archie fire suddenly enfiladed the plane.

Its pilot, however, seemed to be no novice, for he zoomed, leveled off, then dived and banked in such a series of bewildering maneuvers that the anti-aircraft guns found it impossible to follow him.

While Diane and the others watched breathlessly, the pilot headed into the wind and came down on the highway a couple of hundred feet from the barricade, in a perfect three-point landing.

Tim Donovan had left old Captain Allen, and he came over to where Diane was standing with Colonel Givens, Wilstach,

Grogan, Satterly and Marie Joyce. "That looks like one of those fast Boeings," the boy told Diane, "that Jimmy ordered rebuilt and fitted with machine guns. That— say—*look, Di*—" he pointed with a trembling forefinger at the tall, lithe, helmeted and leather-jacketed figure of the aviator who leaped from the cockpit of the Boeing—"if that isn't Jimmy Christopher I'll eat my shirt!"

Diane's face paled and her hand flew to her breast. "Jimmy!" she murmured in a low voice. "It *is* Jimmy."

The aviator raised a hand in greeting, started walking toward them. Now that he had landed, the enemy anti-aircraft guns lapsed once more into silence. A deep quiet seemed to reign over the front, as all the defenders of the barricades watched the lone aviator approach.

Diane turned in panicstricken frenzy to the others. Her slim fingers gripped Colonel Given's arm agitatedly. She burst out into a torrent of speech. "That man is Operator 5—the only man that America looks to, to lead her to salvation. We must not let him become infected with the cholera. If he dies nothing can prevent the Central Empire from marching to the Pacific Ocean. For God's sake, stop him. Keep him at a distance!"

Colonel Givens was the type of man who thought quickly in an emergency. He snapped an order to Captain Grogan: "Take a half-dozen men, Grogan, fix bayonets, and bar his way. And don't let Operator 5 come within ten feet of you!"

GROGAN SWIFTLY selected a half-dozen men and ran at the double-quick to meet Jimmy Christopher. Just beyond the square they halted across the road, presenting a row of gleaming bayonets. Grogan called out sharply: "Halt. Stand where you are. Keep your distance!"

Jimmy Christopher stopped, puzzled. Looking beyond the row of men who barred his way, he could see Diane and Tim and Colonel Givens, whom he knew. Both Diane and Tim avoided looking in his direction. He saw that Diane was talking excitedly to Givens. He frowned, started to say to Grogan: "If this is your idea of a joke—"

Then he stopped abruptly. His quick, comprehending glance had taken in the rows of men and women in the sick-line, and the yellow quarantine flag stuck in a sandbag near the barricade. "Cholera!" he ejaculated. "You've got the cholera here!"

Grogan nodded grimly: "Yes. And you're Operator 5. And we're here to see that you don't come close enough to become infected. We can't spare you yet."

Jimmy motioned impatiently: "Fiddlesticks. I've been inoculated with the antitoxin. I see that Miss Elliot got here, so you must have some serum too. Let me talk to them, man. I didn't fly six hundred miles just for the view."

Grogan turned to look for instructions toward Colonel Givens. The colonel was listening intently to what Diane was saying to him. "Remember, Colonel," she was urging forcefully, "under no circumstances must we let Operator 5 suspect our plan to counterattack. It's just the kind of suicidal thing he'd jump at. We must make some pretext to get rid of him as quickly as possible, before the hour is up!"

Givens nodded his understanding, took Diane's arm, and with Tim and the others following, he came forward to talk to Jimmy Christopher.

Jimmy called out: "Hello, Di. Hello, Tim. How are you, Colonel Givens?" He took an impulsive step forward, but was met by six immovable points of steel centered at his chest. "Damn it!" he exclaimed. "Let me through. What are you hiding here?"

Diane Elliot's face was a study in mental agony. "Oh, Jimmy!" she called. It was evident that she yearned to run to him, to allow him to clasp her in his arms as young Satterlee had done with Marie Joyce a short while before. But Satterlee and Marie were individuals. If they wished to find happiness together in a common death, that was their privilege. To Jimmy Christopher and herself, however, even the privilege of dying together was denied; for the life of Operator 5 did not belong to Diane Elliot, or even to himself—until he had completed the work to which he had dedicated himself.

It was Colonel Givens who took the burden of explanation from Diane. "Please do not misunderstand our action in keeping you at a distance, Operator 5. We are actuated solely by a desire to preserve your life, which is valuable to the country. You see, we have discovered, through Doctor Styles here, that the serum which is being used is no good. The type of cholera with which we are afflicted is not the ordinary one, and until a proper serum can be found, there is no cure or preventive for the plague!"

For a moment there was silence. Then Jimmy said softly: "I see!" His somber eyes found those of Diane, across the line of bayonets, then traveled to Tim Donovan. The two people he loved most in the world were doomed, according to Givens' statement.

"You see, Jimmy," Diane said earnestly, "why you must go? Please, Jimmy, go at once. Tell them in the laboratories that they must work out a new antitoxin. Make them hurry. Perhaps you can do something in time to—save us." She knew, even as she spoke, that it was hopeless. The plague had its grip on them all there, and they were doomed.

Jimmy Christopher, too, understood what Baron Flexner had meant by his parting challenge. Now it was plain why the Baron had said they must surrender unconditionally. His hands clenched at his sides. "I'll go back," he said hollowly. "But I want to take one of you with me. I want to make blood tests. I want to find a new serum. Who will come?"

He looked at Diane, then at Tim. But he knew instinctively that neither would offer to come. And he did not ask them. There was one logical person to go, and they all knew it.

"I think," Colonel Givens said slowly, "that Doctor Styles is the man to return with you. His medical knowledge, coupled with his first-hand experience here, should prove valuable. And he will know how to protect others from infection."

In a few minutes Doctor Styles was ready. He equipped himself with a gauze mask, and prepared one for Jimmy Christopher to wear under his helmet. Also he took from his surgical supplies two pairs of rubber gloves for himself and Jimmy.

"I'm ready," he said simply.

Jimmy Christopher sighed. He was reluctant to go. From the attitudes of Diane and Tim, he suspected that there was some other thing in the wind that they were keeping from him. "I saw the demolished trucks in the road," he said. "There weren't many of your column that got through, were there, Di?"

"No," she told him dully. "Only fifty of us."

"But why have the enemy ceased their bombardment? You are exposed here. If they should begin again—"

"They won't begin again, Jimmy. They are waiting for their bacteria to do the job. But you must fool them. You must develop a new serum!"

Doctor Styles shook hands with Givens and the others, donned his gauze mask and gloves, and joined Jimmy, to whom he handed the second mask and set of gloves. Jimmy sighed, said: "Well, good-bye, Di. Good-bye, Tim."

Tim Donovan forced a cheery smile. "So long, Jimmy. Get to work. Be seeing you soon!"

Diane gulped. "Good-bye, Jimmy. And remember that—" she glanced defiantly around at the crowd, flushed, but went on steadily—"that I—love you!"

For a second Jimmy Christopher's eyes glowed, then he swung on his heel and strode toward the plane, with Styles running to keep up with him.

In silence they all watched him take off, fly to the north. The enemy guns did not open up on him this time, for some unknown reason. Perhaps they thought it better to allow the Boeing to carry back its load of cholera bacteria. If the Central

Empire gunners had shot that plane down, they would have changed the course of history....

Back at the barricades, they watched the Boeing grow smaller and smaller until it became only a speck on the horizon, then disappeared from sight. Colonel Givens heaved a sigh of relief.

"Now," he said, "we can proceed with the attack. Take your stations. Be prepared to go over the top at the whistle!"

A buzz of activity invaded the square. Tim Donovan and Diane shook hands solemnly. "May God forgive me for deceiving Jimmy!" she said, low-voiced. Then abruptly, she clasped Tim Donovan to her breast, kissed him on the forehead, and hurried away to take charge of the women's contingent.

Tim Donovan looked after her with a suspicion of moisture in his eyes. He wiped the back of his hand across his face, gulped, and hurried over to Satterlee, to whose group he had been assigned. "Reporting for orders, sir," he said in a steady voice.

It lacked twelve minutes of the hour's grace they had been granted....

CHAPTER 4
"—BUT NEVER SURRENDERS!"

A S THE sun rose over the arid plains of Arizona, the powerful twin-motored Boeing sped northward, away from Phoenix. Jimmy Christopher, at the controls in the forward cockpit, stared grimly ahead, while Doctor Styles, behind him, peered over the side at the terrain below.

They were flying close behind the front now, and to their right they could see the long lines of trenches, occupied by hastily recruited volunteers just like those who manned the barricades at Phoenix. Beyond the American dugouts, they could see the Central Empire lines, could see the wisps of smoke that curled from hundreds of artillery pieces far behind those lines. A few enemy planes were up, but these confined themselves mainly to observation. Since the oil supply had been curtailed by the destruction of the most important fields in the southwest, the Central Empire was using very few airplanes until fresh supplies could be brought across the ocean from Mesopotamia. They relied mainly on their heavy guns and their tanks to blast the Americans out of the trenches.

Jimmy Christopher's thoughts went inevitably back to the two he had left behind at Phoenix. He entertained few illusions of ever seeing Tim or Diane alive again. The news that the serum was ineffective against this new type of cholera had come as a shock to him. It meant that all the towns already infected—Salt Lake City, Helena, Spokane, Seattle—would become charnel houses of misery and death. And if the rigid quarantines established about those cities should be broken, then this incurable plague would sweep across the entire section of the country still in the hands of the American defenders.

It occurred to Jimmy that Rudolph's executive staff was taking a long chance in using the bacteria, for there was likewise danger of the infection spreading to the Central Empire troops. Such a thing cannot be confined merely to the intended victims. There were inevitably prisoners taken, towns occupied. Germs would spread to the armies of Rudolph, unless—and this idea brought him up sharp—*unless the Central Empire bacteriologists had evolved an effective antitoxin!*

If he could lay hands on the formula for that antitoxin, granting that it existed, the plague might be checked!

His attention was diverted from these thoughts by Doctor Styles' hand tapping him on the back. He turned, saw the doctor pointing excitedly toward the east. Jimmy glanced in that direction, and his eyes narrowed at sight of the drama which was being enacted below them, just behind the American trenches.

One of the vicious little Central Empire light-armored baby tanks had effected a breach in the American line, and was rumbling across the broken country directly toward a tent on a low rise, where a red cross sign indicated the presence of an American field hospital. The American defenders were retreating before the inexorable advance of the tank, and were being mowed down *en masse* by the withering fire from its two turret guns. The tank was advancing directly toward the field hospital!

Jimmy Christopher banked sharply and flew in a wide circle over the tank. His eyes flashed angrily. "Those fools!" he muttered. "Why don't they set off the mines?" He had personally devised a system of mines behind the trenches as the only possible system of defense against tank attack. Sticks of dynamite had been laid at strategic spots, and wired to detonators. Instructions had been issued to all defenders to retreat before tank attack until the monsters should pass over a mined area, and that the mines should then be exploded. Outside of a direct hit by a heavy shell, this was the only way of stopping a tank.

Now, Jimmy Christopher's gaze swung toward the rear, where he saw a group of men clustered about a detonator several hundred yards behind the field hospital. As Jimmy watched, one of the men depressed the handle of the detonator, and they all stood still, waiting for the explosion. It was apparent that the tank was at that moment passing over the mined area.

But nothing happened.

Jimmy bit his lip in an agony of vexation. Something had gone wrong; defective wiring, perhaps. The charge of dynamite had not gone off, and the tank was advancing unmolested directly toward the hospital, its two turret guns vomiting death. Even as he watched from above, Jimmy saw the turret of the tank open.

A Central Empire soldier appeared, beside a peculiar, short-barreled stubby gun that seemed to rise on a platform from within.

Jimmy Christopher recognized this for the new, deadly type of flamethrower lately employed by Rudolph's forces. He knew what that meant. In a moment that stubby gun would hurl a whining projectile that would burst into a hot sheet of flame when it struck the hospital tent. The whole tent would flare into a mass of roaring flame, and every patient within it would be consumed in the fire. It was one of the diabolical devices by means of which Rudolph expected to break the morale of the American Defense Force.

Now the Central Empire soldier swung the flamethrower around on its swivel base, so that its stubby muzzle was pointing directly at the hospital. The man's hand rested on a short lever which would fire the flamethrower. An officer had mounted into view on the turret, and the soldier was apparently only awaiting the officer's order before depressing the lever.

THEN JIMMY CHRISTOPHER sprang into action. He pressed the stick down, and opened the throttle wide. The powerful Boeing vibrated in every strut and joint as it catapulted

He intended to drop the gas shell into the small opening of the turret!

downward in a reckless, roaring power dive, straight at the tank. The Central Empire officer glanced upward for the first time, and noticed the Boeing. He had paid no attention to it until now, for the sight of an American plane at the Front had become a thing of the past. He had naturally assumed, without bothering to verify his assumption, that the ship was one of the Central Empire forces. Now the man's eyes widened in consternation as he glimpsed the American insignia on the fuselage, and as he saw the rack of bombs slung underneath.

He motioned swiftly to the soldier at the gun, and they both dived into the turret. But the turret could not be closed until the flamethrower had descended on its platform. And by that time Jimmy had leveled off, not twenty feet above the tank. His whole body was taut, concentrated on the ticklish thing he had now to do. His hand poised above the row of buttons on the dashboard which controlled the bomb racks beneath, his fore-finger touching the button marked: *"Gas shell."*

This had to be a matter of the most accurate timing, a thing of split seconds. He intended to try to drop the gas shell *into the small opening of the turret!* In order to do that he must judge his speed to the thousandth of a second, must judge his distance without the slightest bit of error or leeway. Moving at a speed of more than a mile and a half a minute, he must release that gas bomb at the exact second which would bring it into the small radius of the turret opening. It was a well-nigh impossible feat, but one that might succeed once in a thousand attempts. And the laws of chance are peculiar in that the first attempt in a thousand-to-one chance might be the successful one just as well as the thousandth.

It cannot be said that Jimmy Christopher consciously went through this process of reasoning in the infinitesimal fraction of time at his disposal. Rather, the accumulation of experience which was his made his actions instinctive rather than the product of reasoning. It is this faculty for quick action which distinguishes men who have thought much on many subjects. The effect of such thought on the mental processes in times of stress is to produce instantaneous action, which often appears to be blind luck.

It is not blind luck. Rather, it is an assurance resulting from prior reasoning; mental preparedness.

Jimmy pressed the button, held his breath as the plane screamed above the tank. He could not know whether the mechanism below the fuselage had responded to his pressure, could not know whether the shell had been released or not. The two forward turret guns had been raised almost perpendicular, and they were spraying lead upward into the plane. Slugs whistled through the body of the ship, scoring into the sides of the cockpit, crashing into the dashboard. The wings were riddled, and a strut tore with a whining snap.

The plane roared through that hail of lead, cleared the tank. It was all over in the wink of an eye. Jimmy Christopher fought the stick, picked the ship up, and banked around. He looked over toward the tank, and his heart sank. He had missed!

He could see where the shell had struck the edge of the turret and had exploded. The brownish side of the tank was discolored, but that was all. Fragments of the shell were still flying in the air, and a dark haze was spreading around the turret opening, where the gas was dispersing itself. But none of that gas was entering the tank.

The stubby flamethrower was still descending, and a head appeared in the turret opening alongside it. It was the Central Empire officer who had jumped below. Now the officer peered over the top, and as he did so, the gas in the air struck his lungs, and he keeled over, slumped, and drooped from sight.

A score of the Americans were now rushing at the tank, shouting, with bayoneted guns. They had been afforded a moment's respite by the raising of the turret guns to shoot at the plane, and now they were advancing to attack the tank.

Jimmy was taking altitude, with the torn strut flapping in the wind. He knew that those Americans would be met by the fumes of the gas and bowled over before they could reach the turret. He leveled off, pushed the stick down, and banked sharply, diving once more toward the tank. The Americans stopped, staring upward, and in that moment Jimmy passed once more close above the metal monster. He did not drop another bomb. The one he had dropped had been the only gas shell he carried, and to drop one of the explosive bombs was useless, since they were constructed differently from the gas shell. They were built so that they turned nose downward in falling, detonating by concussion on the nose. They needed at least five hundred feet clearance.

His purpose was a different one this time. As he passed over the tank, heading for the Americans, the slipstream from his propellers drove a powerful current of air backward, and effectually dissipated the clouds of gas which had formed around the tank, thus leaving the way clear for the Americans. He passed over their heads, waved down to them, and they understood the purpose of his maneuver. With a shout they plunged forward, swarming over the tank and leaping into the turret opening.

Jimmy smiled. The crew of that tank would stand no chance against their desperate onslaught. He straightened out, headed into the wind, and came down to land almost alongside the tank, fighting to keep the broken strut from tilting the plane. But just as he hit the ground, his right hand wing buckled up, and the plane veered sharply, tipped, and dug its nose toward the ground.

There was a splintering crash, and Jimmy Christopher yanked the stick back hard. He righted the plane, braked on one wheel, and brought it to a halt in a wide circle. He looked ruefully over the side. The entire undercarriage was smashed. That plane would not fly again until it had undergone considerable repairs. **JIMMY TURNED** toward the rear cockpit, and drew in his breath sharply. Doctor Styles was sitting slumped over in his seat, a broad ribbon of blood seeping out of a wound in the left side of his chest. Jimmy could see where the bullet, which must have ranged upward, had come out through his shoulder. He must have been hit in that vicious barrage from the tank as they flew overhead.

Styles raised his head with an effort, and his eyes flickered. "Did—we make it?" he mumbled.

Jimmy just barely understood his words, for the doctor's mouth was covered by the antiseptic gauze. "We missed," he told the doctor, "but it gave the boys a chance to rush the tank. They captured it. There they are now, coming out of the turret with the prisoners."

He managed to lift Styles out of the cockpit and lay him on the ground, and in a moment they were surrounded by the victorious Americans, patting Jimmy on the back, dancing with joy. It was so long since they had enjoyed even a minor victory that they were elated beyond the bounds of reason.

Operator 5 paid them no attention, however. He was tearing away the clothing from Doctor Styles' wound, disregarding the danger of cholera infection from the man. Styles pushed him away feebly. "Don't—come near me. I'm—gone anyway!"

Jimmy rapped out over his shoulder: "Bring an operating table out here from the field hospital. Get a doctor. We can't bring him in there, because he's got cholera. But we've got to operate—"

He stopped, bent low as he saw Styles' lips moving. The doctor was smiling wanly, saying: "Don't—bother with me, Operator 5. I'm no—worse off—than the—others back at Phoenix. They—they'll be all dead—in a little while—too."

"Don't you worry, Doc," Jimmy told him heartily. "We'll operate on you, and then I'll work out a serum for the cholera. We'll save you, and those others back at Phoenix—"

Styles was shaking his head. "Too—late—to save—them.

They're going to—launch a suicide attack against the enemy trenches. All—want to die—so as not to spread the—cholera."

"What's that, Doc?" Jimmy bent down tensely, to catch the other's low whisper. "You say they're going to attack? Is that why they were anxious for me to go?"

Styles nodded. "Yes. All—plan to die. Miss Elliot—didn't want you—to stop—them!"

There was a rattle in the doctor's throat, he stiffened, and his jaw opened. His eyes glazed. He was dead.

Slowly Jimmy stood up, cast dark eyes on the wrecked plane. He was less than twenty miles from Phoenix. But the plane would never make it—wouldn't even take off.

The jubilant Americans surrounding him had quieted abruptly when they saw that Doctor Styles was dead. A young reserve lieutenant, hardly more than eighteen, came up to Jimmy. "We all want to thank you, sir, for giving us the opportunity to capture that tank. They'd have set fire to our field hospital. If there's anything we can do for you—"

Jimmy interrupted anxiously. "I've got to get back to Phoenix at once. My plane's crippled. Have you got any kind of transportation?"

The young lieutenant shook his head regretfully. "Not a thing, sir. Since the gasoline shortage, all motorcycles and cars have been called in from the front. We use runners—"

Suddenly, Jimmy Christopher's eyes flashed. He exclaimed: "The tank! I can use that! Those baby tanks will make fifty miles an hour!"

The lieutenant smiled. "Why, sure, sir! It's a natural!"

They did not know that Jimmy was Operator 5. But they did not question him. They had seen him in action over that tank, and they instinctively knew he was one to obey. A dozen of them rushed to the tank, dragged out the dead bodies of two Americans and two Central Empire troopers who had died in the scrimmage, and got the interior ready.

Jimmy shook hands with the lieutenant, pulled down the Central Empire flag from the turret and substituted the stars and stripes which they gave him. In a few moments he was ready to go. Two of the men volunteered to accompany him to man the guns in case they should meet enemy patrols, and Jimmy himself took the controls. They set out southward once more, leaving Doctor Styles' pitiful body to be buried there.

As he faced toward Phoenix, Jimmy's lips moved in fervent prayer. "God grant that I reach them in time!"

CHAPTER 5
TUNNEL TO DOOM

WHILE OPERATOR 5 was racing madly across the arid Arizona plains in a desperate attempt to forestall the suicidal sacrifice of the cholera victims at Phoenix, a drama of a far different nature was taking place several hundred miles to the north, in the city of Denver.

Emperor Rudolph I, Master of the Central Empire, had commandeered the spacious United States Mint Building here for his headquarters. The main floor had been stripped of its office equipment; costly furniture, rugs and pictures, confiscated from American stores, had been substituted. The army staff occupied another section of the building, while the entire upper floor had been gutted and re-equipped as a laboratory. Here, strange experiments were being conducted under the utmost secrecy. No one was admitted to this floor without a pass from either the Emperor or Baron Flexner.

Men whispered of dreadful things that took place here. It was known that many Americans, residents of the city and adjacent neighborhood, had been brought up there as prisoners, and had never been heard from again. Truckloads of chemical equipment and cases of pharmaceutical supplies had been delivered to the building and gone up in the elevator to the top floor. And other cases, containing small vials of amber-colored liquid, were shipped out of there, marked for delivery to the officers in charge of the various units of the Imperial Army at the front and in all parts of the occupied territory.

All this queer activity mystified and frightened the residents of Denver. And then it began to be rumored that there, on the top floor of the Mint, were being produced the bacteria which the Imperial Army was using to spread the cholera infection among the American cities. And men whispered to each other that the Americans who were brought there were being used as human cultures for these bacteria!

All this news was spread by the grapevine telegraph which had somehow sprung up among the residents of the occupied territory. For there were no longer any newspapers, and there was a curfew law in every occupied city forbidding anyone to be in the streets after eight o'clock in the evening—on pain of instant execution. Swaggering Central Empire troopers patrolled the streets and delighted in practicing their marksmanship on any unfortunates whom they found violating the curfew law.

Every morning, fresh bodies were found in the streets, lying pitifully crumpled where they had been shot; and relatives stole out furtively to cart away those bodies for burial, fearful lest they be arrested in the very process of caring for their dead.

Rudolph's sycophantic courtiers modeled their attitude upon that of their master. They stood at the windows of the converted U.S. Mint Building and made jokes among themselves at the expense of a middle-aged man and woman in the street outside. These two, weary and haggard from a night of anxiety, were lifting the body of a young man into a wheelbarrow. It was apparent to Rudolph and his courtiers that these two elderly people were the young man's parents. Blood spattered the dead boy's body and there was a gaping hole in the back of his head where a trooper's rifle bullet had caught him.

The body had been lying since sunrise in the angle of an alley running alongside the old Union Hotel, which was directly opposite the Mint.

In the spacious room which had been set aside as Rudolph's Chamber of State, there were present in addition to the dozen or so courtiers at the windows the Emperor himself, Baron Flexner, and half a dozen members of the Emperor's personal entourage. Rudolph and Flexner had the center window to themselves while the others crowded around the two flanking windows.

Outside, the sun was slowly warming up the cold, crisp Denver air. A company of the Tenth Imperial Hussars, Rudolph's personal bodyguard, was drawn up before the door of the building. Other Central Empire troopers in steel helmets and gray greatcoats were moving about in the street. The few civilians who passed gave the troopers a wide berth, and appeared not to be looking at the pitiful sight of the two elderly people, who had just succeeded in getting the dead boy's body into the wheelbarrow. The man picked up the shafts of the barrow and began slowly to wheel it down the street, while the woman walked at his side pressing a small handkerchief against her mouth. These two were typical of the millions of American parents throughout the land who writhed under the heel of the conqueror, who were forced to stand by helpless and see their daughters ravished and their sons murdered by the ruthless servants of the Purple Emperor.

Now, as they moved away with their beloved burden, the elderly man's shoulders seemed to sag under the weight of his sorrow, while the mother's body was racked with sobs. This thing that had happened to their son was neither unexpected nor avoidable. In hundreds of American cities young men just like this one had been caught within the occupied territory by the swift advance of the Purple troops and were unable to join the American Defense Force. So they braved the curfew laws as this one had done, and went out into the night to secret meetings of patriots, where they plotted and planned the eventual deliverance of their country.

And every night some of them failed to run the gantlet of the Central Empire sentries. Now this one's parents were taking him away to an unassuming grave.

But before the funeral procession had gone ten feet beyond the old Union Hotel, Rudolph, from his window in the Chamber of State, intervened. With a twisted, sadistic smile he turned to Baron Flexner, who stood at his elbow. "Those two old people, my dear Flexner," he said, "are very miserable. I shall end their misery!" And, leaning out of the window, he motioned to the officer in charge of the Imperial Hussars in the street below. That officer showed his teeth in a cruel smile, and bowed low from the waist. Then, snapping erect, he barked a series of staccato orders at his troops. The first rank of soldiers dropped to one knee, raised rifles to shoulder and sighted at the aged couple. The second rank aimed over the heads of the first. The two elderly people proceeded with their funereal load, unaware of the peril which threatened them from behind—the officer's sabre flashed out of its scabbard, and he raised it high in the air, then brought it down with a swoop. "Fire!" he commanded.

A ROARING salvo burst from the guardsmen's guns. The street reverberated to the crashing echoes of the volley, and the aged couple crumpled over the dead body of their son, riddled by the hail of bullets.

At their officer's command, the Hussars stood back at attention, and the officer looked up toward Rudolph, who nodded and smiled in approbation. With calloused indifference a detail of troopers emerged from a side door of the Mint Building and carted away the three pitiful bodies.

In the Chamber of State the courtiers were chattering with cynical gayness about the bloody spectacle. Several of them came over and subserviently congratulated Rudolph on his cleverness in staging the double killing.

Baron Flexner was the only one who remained silent. That tall, gaunt man stood at the Emperor's side and said not a word, until Rudolph turned to him, frowning.

"And you, Flexner? You do not seem to have found pleasure, like these others, in our little spectacle? Judging by your sour expression, it would even seem that you do not approve!" There was a dangerous coldness in the Emperor's voice—the same cold, merciless tone which made his courtiers shiver when they heard it. For when Rudolph spoke this way, the Emperor was angry, and men who incurred the Emperor's anger died surely and painfully.

But Flexner was no ordinary courtier. Shrewd, clever, as ruthless and as conscienceless as his master, he had become invaluable as Rudolph's confidential adviser.

"If I appear to disapprove, Your Imperial Majesty," he said suavely, "it is because your best interests lie always in my mind. As for the deed itself, it was nothing. These fools deserve no better."

Rudolph's brows furrowed as he frowned in a puzzled manner. "I do not understand you, Flexner," he rasped. "If you approve of the act, how can you also disapprove? And what have my best interests to do with a little innocent sport like this?"

Flexner lowered his voice. "Allow me to explain, Sire. These Americans are a peculiar people. As you know, I have just returned from delivering your ultimatum to Z-7 and Operator 5 in San Francisco. I explained to them the hopelessness of further resistance. I showed them that the Imperial Armies could not be stopped, and that the cholera would finish any work of extermination that we have begun. And what do you think, Sire, they answered?"

Flexner paused dramatically for a moment, then went on as Rudolph listened with avidity. "They merely laughed at me, Sire! It is this quality of the Americans that I cannot understand. The greater our harshness, the greater the punishment we inflict upon them, the more stubborn does their resistance become. That is why I wonder whether it is wise to continue these oppressive measures."

Rudolph demanded: "What would you have me do, Flexner?"

"Perhaps, Sire, if we were to appear to become more lenient we could lull these American fools into a false sense of security. Later, we could crush them—"

Rudolph laughed harshly. "No! I might perhaps do this that you suggest, my dear Baron, but for one thing. As long as Operator 5 is free I shall have no mercy for the Americans. That man has flouted me a dozen times, and until I have had the pleasure of listening to his screams of anguish on the torture rack there shall be no leniency for Americans!"

"Perhaps, Sire—" Flexner's smile became wily—"it may be possible to strike an indirect blow at Operator 5—through one whom he loves very much."

Rudolph's eyes narrowed. "What do you mean, Flexner?"

For answer the Baron produced from his pocket a sheet of paper. "As you know, Sire, the Americans already suspect that we are developing the cholera bacteria in the laboratory upstairs. I have discovered that Operator 5's twin sister, Nan, is in hiding here in Denver with a small band of Americans and Canadians. They are planning to gain entrance to this building in order to destroy the laboratory.

"In Denver?" Rudolph exclaimed excitedly. "Where in Denver? How do you know this?"

Flexner's smile broadened. "On the flight back from San Francisco, Sire, we spied a carrier pigeon flying westward. We shot it down, and landed and recovered the message it was bearing. That message was in the old Z Code, which our cryptographers had already broken down. Here, Sire, is the translation!" He handed over the second of the two messages which Nan had sent to Z-7 by carrier pigeon. The thing that Jimmy Christopher had foreseen and feared had come to pass. Nan's presence in the Union Hotel was known to the Purple Emperor.

Rudolph was literally trembling with diabolic joy. "The Union Hotel!" he exclaimed. "Flexner, you have done well. You shall be rewarded beyond your fondest dreams. We will arrest this sister of Operator 5 at once, and make her wish that she had never been born!"

Flexner was doubtful. "I have already had the building searched, Sire. A dozen of our best undercover men are in it this very moment, but they have not been able to locate either the girl or her companions. As you know, all our staff officers are quartered there. The hotel is devoted exclusively to members of the army and of the Imperial household who cannot be accommodated in this building."

"But this message, Flexner—she distinctly says: 'We have a

hideout in the old Union Hotel, where the Purple Emperor will never find us in a thousand years.' They must be somewhere in the building—"

"It may be, Sire, that there is a secret chamber somewhere in the building." Flexner's eyes strayed out of the window toward the ancient structure of the Union Hotel directly opposite. "It is a very old building. There may be some unsuspected space between the walls or in the cellar—"

The Emperor's eyes were flashing. "We shall soon discover if there is, Flexner. Order the hotel vacated. Let everyone move. Send in a company of engineers. Have them tear down the building, brick by brick, and wall by wall. If that girl and her companions are in there, we shall find them!"

The Baron bowed low and backed away.

"I obey, Your Imperial Majesty!" he murmured....

THE UNION HOTEL, across the street, seemed faded and worn and drab by comparison with the modern, new buildings that surrounded it. Built in 1902, its outmoded cornices and its long, musty bay windows peered out at the glittering newness of the city with the shy diffidence of a bygone day. Not so long ago, it had been one of Denver's cheaper commercial hotels. Now, because of its nearness to the building where Rudolph had established his headquarters, it was peopled by gaily uniformed, swaggering officers, and insolent courtiers. In the kitchen and dining room, American civilians, working under the forced labor decree recently issued by Rudolph, were preparing food for these arrogant conquerors.

Here and there, in the corridors and in the basement, cunning fox-eyed men moved about tapping walls, prying partitions, and measuring off distances. These were undercover men, members of the Surveillance Department of the Purple Empire. They were the men whom Flexner had sent into the building to discover Nan's hiding-place. They moved about in the cellar, poking into the outmoded furnace in one corner, and examining the new oil burner nearby which had been installed to replace the furnace.

If any of those men had accidentally stepped upon a certain section of the floor behind the furnace, and at the same time placed his hand upon a dirty coal spot on the wall, he would have been startled to find that the old furnace was slowly moving, as if on a pivot. And if he had watched closely—as he undoubtedly would have done—he would have seen a dark, circular opening in the floor directly beneath the spot where the furnace had stood. Lowering himself into this opening, the investigator would have found an iron-runged ladder to facilitate his descent. Upon reaching the bottom of that ladder, he would have found himself in a huge, square chamber cut into the rock, and abutting upon the stone wall of the Denver sewage system.

However, none of those investigators had the happy thought of trying to move the ancient furnace. And the occupants of that chamber were so far undiscovered. Those occupants consisted of one woman and ten men.

The woman was young, fair-haired, and beautiful even in the flickering light of the half-dozen candles resting on the floor. In a better light one might have noted the startling resemblance which she bore to Operator 5. She was, indeed, his twin sister, Nan Christopher. At the moment she was seated on a wooden box, the only piece of furniture in the chamber. Five of the ten men were resting on the floor, and they were all carrying on a low-voiced, animated conversation.

The ventilation here was very poor, coming as it did from several vent holes which had been bored into the side wall abutting on the sewer. The wall opposite Nan was not solid. In its center, and rising about three feet from the floor, was the opening of a tunnel from which came the sounds of men's voices and of tools being cautiously wielded.

Of the five men who were seated on the floor of the chamber, one was a small, wizened individual of about forty. This man's eyes, though small and shrewd, appeared to be constantly laughing. His hands were long and thin, and his fingers might have been those of a great musician—or of a successful pickpocket. This man's name was Slips McGuire. And he had in fact, at one time, been a member of the light-fingered gentry who made their living in the crowded subways of New York. All that was past now, however, and Slips McGuire now devoted his peculiar talents and his experience in the criminal world to the service of his country.

Nan Christopher was saying to him: "I still don't understand, Slips, how you came to know that there was a hidden chamber under this hotel. If it weren't for this spot, we would have been caught by the Purple Guards long ago!"

Slips McGuire grinned sheepishly. "Well, Miss Nan, you see, it's like this." He threw a glance around at the other men seated on the floor, seemed to hesitate, shrugged, and then went on defiantly: "Before I threw in with Operator 5, I was a crook. I guess you fellows know about that. Well, I knew all the big-timers and I knew what was going on. John Carrone, the big-shot racketeer, bought this place about a year ago and did a little remodeling on it. He built this chamber down here and he started that tunnel. His idea was to tunnel under the street and work up right alongside the elevator shaft of the Mint. That's the only spot in the building where they haven't got a three-foot concrete wall. Can you imagine the haul Carrone would have made—with a private entrance into the United States Mint?"

The other four men and Nan Christopher were listening closely. Nan asked: "What happened to the plan, Slips? Didn't Carrone go through with it?"

McGuire shook his head mournfully. "You know how Carrone got arrested for income tax evasion and sent to Alcatraz. This chamber and the tunnel stayed just the way they were left. Nobody in Carrone's outfit had the guts to go ahead with it. But everybody in the underworld knew all about the stunt.

I guess—" he grinned shyly—"the only ones who didn't know about it were the Denver police. I figure—"

He stopped as a rumbling movement came from the tunnel and five dirty, begrimed men filed out, carrying pickaxes and shovels.

Nan Christopher got up eagerly and addressed one of these men: "How does it look, Sergeant MacTavish?"

MacTAVISH WAS a tall, dark-haired Canadian, who had been a sergeant of the Royal Canadian Mounted Police before the Purple Invasion had swept across Canada and the United States. Nan had contacted him and these other Canadians, and they had volunteered to assist her in this undertaking.*

MacTavish put down his pickaxe and grinned through the

---

* AUTHOR'S NOTE: Regular readers of these chronicles of the exploits of Operator 5 and the Purple Invasion will readily recall having met Slips McGuire before. His peculiar gifts have been of inestimable assistance to Operator 5 in the past. It will be recalled that in the early stages of the Purple Invasion (described in the August–September issue entitled "Patriots' Death Battalion") when Operator 5 lay prisoner in a lonely dungeon, betrayed to the enemy by traitors within our own ranks, it was Slips McGuire who used his knowledge of wire-tapping to discover Jimmy Christopher's whereabouts. On many other occasions has this shy little man given evidence to Operator 5's perspicacity in taking him out from the morass of crime into the service of the country. Now, too, we see how Slips McGuire's knowledge of the going on in the underworld had become useful for a lawful purpose.

coating of dust that covered his face. "We're practically finished, Miss Christopher," he announced triumphantly. "We've tunneled right up to the walls of the elevator shaft, and all we've got to do now is cut through it—about an hour's work. These boys—" he indicated McGuire and the other seated men—"can relieve us now and start cutting through—"

It was at this moment that a strange sound of hammering and crashing came to their ears from above. They all looked at one another questioningly. Sergeant MacTavish said: "Sounds like queer doings up there. Let's have a look." He mounted the iron ladder and opened a small peep-hole directly in front of the sliding trapdoor in the ceiling. This peep-hole was placed directly in front of the furnace in the cellar above. And by applying his eye to it, he could see men moving around in the lighted cellar, could hear their conversation. He frowned in puzzlement, and descended.

"I can't see much in there, Miss Christopher," he said, "but there's a lot of men in the cellar and they're talking in that foreign language of theirs. And I can't understand a word of it."

"I speak the language," Nan said hurriedly. She brushed by him and climbed the ladder. Distinctly now she could hear the voices of two men. She did not know it at the time, but one of those men was Baron Flexner. He was speaking to the captain in command of the engineer company. "Your men, Captain, are not tearing down the building fast enough to suit His Imperial Highness. The Emperor cannot wait all day. He is impatient to find the girl."

"I am very sorry, Herr Baron," the captain said regretfully. "My men are demolishing the building as fast as they can—"

"It is not fast enough!" the Baron rapped. "The Emperor wishes to take more drastic steps. You will lay a charge of dynamite here in the cellar, and set it off at once. The Emperor wishes to see the whole building come down in ruins. If the girl and her band are hiding here, they will be destroyed!"

"B-but, Herr Baron, that may weaken the foundations of neighboring buildings—"

"What of it? Have we not destroyed whole cities in this land? What are a few buildings? It is an Imperial order, Captain. Let us have no delay. The Emperor is watching from his window. He wishes to see this hotel dynamited within the next ten minutes. Hurry!"

"It—it shall be done, Herr Baron!"

As the voices of the Baron and the captain died away, Nan Christopher moved down the ladder with the speed of panic. "Slips! Mac!" she exclaimed in a hushed, urgent voice.[*]

The two men, seeing her wide eyes and her heaving breast, hurried to her side, sensing crisis. She told them swiftly the gist of the conversation she had overheard, while the other men grouped around them.

---

[*] AUTHOR's NOTE: For details of the thrilling circumstances under which Nan Christopher met Sergeant MacTavish the reader is referred to the novel entitled "The Bloody Forty-five Days."

Slips McGuire whistled. "Boy! So they've discovered that we're hiding somewhere in the hotel. Must have been one of your pigeon messages, Nan." He smiled proudly. "Anyway, they couldn't find this subcellar—"

"Yeah," MacTavish broke in. "But that doesn't do us any good. According to what Nan heard, they're going to lay a charge of dynamite in this building inside of ten minutes. You know what that means?"

"The building'll come down—"

"Right. And we'll be buried under the explosion. The cellar will cave in on us. We'll be crushed—"

"Good Lord! We better get in the tunnel—"

MacTavish shook his head. "No good, Slips. The debris would choke up the tunnel, and we'll be smothered alive. We've got to do more than that. *We've got to break through the elevator shaft in ten minutes!*" He gripped his pick, rapped out the names of two of the men. "Come on, Joslin and Calvert. We have work to do!"

THE THREE men pushed into the low tunnel. The others watched them go, helpless to do anything to aid them, for the space at the far end of the tunnel was barely large enough for three men to work in. The others must wait, holding their breath for the explosion from above. MacTavish called back from inside the tunnel: "If we can break through in time, we'll call back to you. If not, then God help us all!"

Nan Christopher was standing rigid in the center of the chamber. Slips McGuire was looking at her in a peculiar way, while the other men grouped together talking in suddenly hushed voices. "I feel just like a miner that's trapped in a shaft," one of them said. "Only the difference is that they try to rescue trapped miners. No one'll try to rescue us!"

Someone else silenced the speaker. "Shut up, you fool! Why don't you pray instead of talking like that!"

The men grew silent. Slips McGuire came close to Nan. "What are you thinking about, Nan?" he asked softly.

She looked at him speculatively. "I'm thinking, Slips, that MacTavish will never be able to break through that shaft in time. We'll all die down here, and our mission will fail."

Slips shrugged fatalistically. "It's the fortune of war, Nan. For myself, I don't care. I'm an old rogue, and no one will lose much by my going. But you—you're young and beautiful, and clever." His eyes flamed in impotent rage. "It's a damned shame, Nan—"

"It's not that, Slips," she said hurriedly. "Don't you see, Slips, that we're the only ones who have even a slight chance of finding out the secret of the Central Empire's bacteriological warfare? We *must* get into the Mint Building. *We must prevent the explosion from taking place!*"

"But how, Nan? If there was a way—"

"There *is* a way, Slips. Rudolph wants to capture me. Don't you see, it's his hate of Jimmy that's driving him to blow up this building. If I were his prisoner, he'd probably cancel the order. Then you and Mac and these other boys could work down here at your leisure, and break through—"

She stopped as the broad figure of Sergeant MacTavish appeared in the tunnel opening. His long face, grimly set, told them that he was bringing bad news. "I'm sorry, folks," he said in a low voice. "It's impossible to break through that shaft in ten minutes. It's a good hour's job. I guess—we're in for it!"

One of the men laughed jerkily. "Three minutes to go."

Nan raised her voice. "Boys, I'm going to stop that explosion. I'm going to give myself up. Then you'll have time to break through!"

They all swung on her. "You'll do nothing of the sort, Nan!" MacTavish roared. "That Rudolph is a fiend. He'd torture you for days—"

"Would you rather," Nan asked sweetly, "have me stay here so that we can all be crushed to death by the explosion? This way, we'll all have a breathing spell!" Determinedly she began to mount the ladder. "Well, good-bye, boys. It's been fun. If I stave off the explosion, start digging away. Maybe they'll keep me prisoner in the Mint Building—then you'll have a chance to get me out of there if you break through."

MacTavish ripped out a low oath, pushed Slips McGuire aside, and rushed toward the ladder. "I won't let you do it, Nan! I can't stand the thought of your body being torn by Rudolph's executioners—"

He brought up short, facing the muzzle of a small revolver, which Nan was leveling at him from above. "Stand where you are, Sergeant MacTavish!" she grated. "If you try to stop me, I swear I'll shoot you!"

MacTavish stared up at her with agony in his eyes. "Nan! For God's sake, don't do it!"

She smiled down at him. "I know how you feel about me,

Mac." Her voice was choked. "It's got to be this way, though. Good-bye."

She pressed the palm of her hand against a spot in the roof, and the trapdoor began to slide open. Hastily, the men below doused the candles, so the light would not be spotted from above. And in the darkness, Nan Christopher passed through the opening, to give herself up.

CHAPTER 6
BLOODY SIEGE

AT ALMOST the same time that Nan Christopher was opening that trapdoor preparatory to sacrificing herself, a gallant company of men and women were making another sacrifice some six hundred miles away.

Along the barricades in the blackened, shell-scarred ruins of Phoenix, the shrill blast of a whistle cut through the dry air. Colonel Givens, standing erect in the center of the square, had given the signal to attack!

At once a low cheer went up, and thirty men arose from behind the barricade. Lieutenant Wilstach raised his hand, and they went over the top, each carrying a submachine gun. Racing through the street, they came out into the open, facing the enemy trenches. Wilstach ran in the lead, and they spread out behind him, running in a crouching position.

From the enemy trenches a blast of machine gun fire blazed out at them. Several of them dropped, thrashing on the ground, riddled by the sudden hail. The others crawled forward on their stomachs, moving forward inch by inch. None of them expected to live for another ten minutes. But they meant to get as close to the enemy lines as they could before they died. Lead pellets from the Central Empire machine-gun barrage kicked up the dirt in their faces, thudded into flesh and bone.

They hugged the ground tightly, while from the barricades behind them a hail of supporting fire was suddenly poured at the enemy trenches. The enemy barrage slowed up under that desperate covering fire, and the gallant crew pushed on. But hardly a dozen of them were still alive. Wilstach himself lay still, the top of his head ripped off by machine-gun slugs. The survivors were close to the objective now. They could see the rounded steel helmets of the enemy, could even see the muzzles of the long rifles that were poked out, vomiting death at them. Now they no longer crouched. They rose to their feet, dropped the submachine guns, and raced forward, each clutching a grenade. Hot lead sank into their flesh, but they came on with the last reserve ounce of energy in their bodies. Of the last dozen, six reached the enemy trenches, hurled their grenades with a last superhuman effort, then dropped.

The grenades burst with muffled detonations, and for a moment the enemy fire was stopped.

Behind them, two shrill blasts of Colonel Givens' whistle had already sounded, and the second wave of two hundred men under Grogan were already charging. Due to the havoc the grenades had done, Grogan's men were able to get within pistol range of the enemy before they were subjected to fire. Then, the troops on either side of the stricken enemy trenches opened up with machine guns, enfilading them from two sides. They began to drop fast. The field became strewn with dead and wounded. Grogan was the first to reach one of the submachine guns dropped by the first wave. He seized it, ran at his full height for perhaps thirty feet with bullets whining all around him. His men came close behind, shouting, yelling frenziedly. And those who picked up machine guns knelt with them, sent a withering fire in answer to the enemy barrage from the adjoining trenches. But the Purple troops were firing at an open field, and they mowed down the charging men like tenpins.

The men seemed to be possessed of a fanatical courage that was almost terrifying. They charged directly into the withering hail of fire, running on after they had been hit many times. A number of them reached the enemy trenches, only to be shot down. In less time than it takes to tell there was not a single one of the two hundred remaining alive.

But the main body was coming.

In the forefront of this last wave, old Captain Allen pushed forward, outstripping Givens and Satterlee, who led the attack. The old man's face was flushed with the excitement of battle, and he seemed to be remembering other engagements in the dim past—other charges where men had fallen. Even now, men were falling on all sides of him, but the old Confederate officer seemed to have a charmed life.

Bullets whined past his frail old body, mowing down men on either side. But none appeared to touch him, for he advanced steadily, standing upright, scorning to seek comparative safety by hugging the ground as many of the others were doing. By now, the enemy riflemen and machine-gunners had recovered from the effects of the grenades, and they were concentrating their fire upon the leaders of the charge.

Colonel Givens stopped short in the act of running, and his body seemed to stiffen, literally to be carried backward by the solid sheet of lead that swept into him. He was hurled to the ground at the feet of the men behind him, his chest virtually shot open. Blood streamed out over his uniform, and he lay staring upward while his men passed around his body, staring intently forward.

NOW MEN were falling on every side. Those behind had to pick their way across the field in order to avoid the bodies of their dead and wounded comrades. But Captain Allen still ran in the van, brandishing in one hand an old army pistol, and in the other a modern grenade. Almost within fifty feet of the enemy dugout, a sniper's bullet caught him in the forehead, and he pitched forward. It seemed to those behind him that his arm moved even after he was dead. For it described a wide arc, and the grenade slipped from his lifeless grip, described a long parabola, and descended within the enemy trench. A spurt of smoke and flame, accompanied by the wicked explosion, followed the landing of the grenade. The men behind him uttered a cheer and swarmed over the top, with young Satterlee in the lead.

The remaining Central Empire soldiers could easily have cut down every one of the gallant attackers in the hand-to-hand fighting which followed, for there was not a single American without at least one wound; and Purple troops from the adjoining trenches on both sides were hurrying over to support their fellows so that the Americans could have been attacked on three sides.

Young Satterlee saw the danger, but before he could do anything about it, he noticed a peculiar thing—the Central Empire troops were giving way before them! In almost a moment the trench which they had stormed was cleared of Purple troopers. And those who had advanced from the adjoining trenches on either side were also retreating. The Americans uttered wild whoops of victory and dashed after them. Satterlee, himself, led a small handful over the top of the first trench deep into enemy territory. Machine guns sputtered at them from hidden nests, but no troops dared to face them in hand-to-hand conflict. Without stopping to seek the reason for this strange phenomenon, Satterlee raced forward at the head of some hundred men who had followed him. They ploughed through converging lanes of machine-gun fire, losing fully half their number before they reached the enemy nests and hurled grenades into them. Now they were close upon the heels of the retreating Purple troopers, and Satterlee suddenly understood why the Emperor's men fled before them, for he heard their frightened voices raised in cries of terror: "The plague! The cholera! They carry the cholera!"

These troopers knew that the embattled Americans carried the cholera infection, and they feared catching the plague more than they feared the wrath of their officers.

Now that the enemy machine-gun nests had been exterminated, the enfilading fire ceased; and Satterlee paused a moment to take toll of their losses. Of the five hundred men who had participated in that third charge there were less than fifty remaining alive in his group. Two other groups totaling possibly another fifty were moving up to join them from the first-line enemy trenches. These men all wore expressions of incredulity and bewilderment tinged with wondering triumph; for they had expected to die in that charge. All of them marveled at the fact that the war-hardened Purple troopers were retreating before them.

Satterlee shouted: "Come on, boys. We've got them on the run. They're afraid of the plague. Let's do as much damage as we can before they finish us!"

But now the enemy began to ring them in. From their left the huge enemy tanks came bearing down upon them, guns spitting flaring death in their direction. They were between the enemy first-line trench and the tanks. The Purple troopers, pouring in from both sides of the breach they had made in the trench, directed a withering rifle fire at them. Men began to drop, writhing in agony as lines of spitting bullets began to plow into them.

Satterlee shouted: "Follow me!" and led them at right angles, away from the advancing tanks. But the tank guns exacted a deadly toll from their number.

Satterlee rushed on, wild-eyed, seeking cover for his men. Ahead, he glimpsed the scarlet tunic of a high Imperial officer, limping away. The man must have been hit by a stray bullet, and he was trying to get out of the path of the rushing Americans. Satterlee leaped at the officer, and abruptly realized that he no longer had his gun, for when he had emptied it in the close fighting in the trench he had flung it at the head of a trooper who was about to bayonet him. He gripped the officer's throat with his bare hands while the officer beat at him desperately with both fists. Satterlee suddenly recognized the man. It was Major Horty, the officer who had brought them the ultimatum only a short while before. The two fought on the ground, while the other Americans streamed past seeking safety from the advancing tanks, which had ceased firing for fear of hitting Major Horty.

Satterlee was fighting desperately, though his strength was rapidly weakening, because there were wounds in his right shoulder and a searing scar across his temple where a bullet had grazed him. To his surprise he found that Horty was not trying to overcome him, but was frantically endeavoring to get away from him.

With a last frantic effort Horty broke the young lieutenant's grip on his throat and got to his feet, started limping away, dragging his wounded leg as best he could. Satterlee, with black dots swimming before his eyes, staggered erect to follow the major. Horty retreated in terror, his face pale, shouting: "The cholera! Don't touch me, for God's sake!" Horty was fumbling in a pocket under his scarlet uniform tunic, and brought out a small vial of dark, muddy-colored liquid. He tore out the cork of this vial and raised the contents to his lips. And at that moment Satterlee dived at him with his last remaining strength in a low football tackle. Horty uttered a shriek and went toppling backwards, the vial flying out of his hand. The two landed in a heap on the ground.

Satterlee picked himself up, with the din of thundering guns still in his ears, wondering why the tanks had not yet caught up with him. His red-rimmed eyes, staring about, filled with sudden anguish as he saw that the remaining men of his command had been mowed down to the last one. Streaming past, they had met a deadly barrage from two tanks which had cut off their retreat. Not a man of them was left alive. A hundred feet behind him the enemy tanks were lumbering in his direction. The sounds of rifle fire and of hand-to-hand combat came to him from the direction of the enemy first-line trench. He blinked his eyes to clear them, and uttered a low oath. There was fighting going on in that trench, yes. "The women!" he exclaimed, "they charged too!"

IT WAS indeed so. The women under Diane, seeing that the end had come for the men, had clamored for a chance to attack. And Diane, with Tim Donovan beside her, had led the charge. Of the seventy-odd women who had gone over the top, only a dozen had reached the enemy dugout. The troopers had given way before them, still fearing the plague. But they were ringed around by a circle of barking rifles and machine guns which would soon exterminate them.

Satterlee glanced about him desperately, glimpsed a bayoneted rifle on the ground which had been abandoned by one of the fleeing Purple troopers. Major Horty had come to his knees, and just as Satterlee started for the rifle, Horty screamed an oath, drew his holstered revolver and fired at the young lieutenant.

Satterlee's lunge for the rifle saved him from that slug. In the next second Satterlee had the rifle gripped in his two hands and lunged at Horty. The bayonet caught the Purple major in the stomach. Horty screamed, dropped his revolver, and sank to the ground. Satterlee twisted the bayonet out of the major's body, uttered a hollow laugh and began staggering in the direction of the front-line trench, where the few surviving women were still fighting.

His foot touched the vial of muddy-colored liquid which Horty had been about to swallow. A few drops of the contents still remained in it, and Satterlee for some reason which he never was able to explain, stooped and picked up the vial. He thrust it into his pocket and swayed on his feet. Now the enemy tanks began to fire once more. They were close upon him now, and Satterlee realized that in another moment he would be cut down. It was at that instant that a small tank of Central Empire construction but, strangely, flying the American flag, streaked across the enemy trench and raced in between Satterlee and the approaching tanks. The turret door sprang open and Satterlee's unbelieving eyes saw the face of Operator 5.

"Come on, boy," Operator 5 called. "In here, quick!"

Satterlee climbed into the tank dizzily, while streams of enemy slugs rapped a mad tattoo against the armored sides. Operator 5, at the controls within the tank, set it in motion once more and swung back toward the trench. The two American gunners within the tank sent a withering stream of fire at the ring of Purple troopers who surrounded Diane, Tim and the few surviving women. The Central Empire soldiers disintegrated before that deadly burst of accurate shooting, and Jimmy Christopher drove the tank headlong through their grim circle, peering out and motioning to the surviving women. He had so maneuvered his tank that it was between the women and the

Six weary, wounded women climbed into the tank followed by Tim Donovan and Diane.

enemy tanks, thus protecting them from the Purple barrage. One after another, six weary, wounded women climbed into the tank. Tim Donovan came next and Diane last.

Jimmy Christopher swung to the steel turret door, and raced the tank back toward Phoenix. Behind them, strung out in a long pursuing line, came the enemy tanks, with guns spitting spitefully but harmlessly against their steel armor. Within the narrow confines of the American tank Diane was tending to the wounds of Satterlee and several of her girl followers. Young Satterlee had lost consciousness upon dropping into the tank. And one of the women who had accompanied Diane was kneeling on the floor, holding the young lieutenant's head in her lap. It was Marie Joyce. There were tears in her eyes, and her lips trembled as she looked up at Diane, who had broken open the tank's first aid kit and was swabbing out Satterlee's wounds.

"W-will he live, Miss Elliot?" Marie demanded tremulously.

"I don't know," Diane said, low-voiced, "but I dearly hope so—for your sake, Marie!"

"And for his own, too!" the voice of Jimmy Christopher interrupted her. He had given over the controls of the tank to Tim Donovan, and now he was stooping over Satterlee's unconscious form, reaching into the lieutenant's pocket for the open vial which protruded from it.

Diane looked up at Operator 5 quizzically. She had been through a dreadful experience, had seen her entire column annihilated by drumfire, had just seen men and women whom she knew and loved shot down in the hopeless charge upon the Purple trenches. And now the man whom she loved more than anyone else in the world had appeared when everything seemed to be lost, and had snatched her from certain death. Yet such was her poise that no inane word of greeting or of thanks came to her lips. In the deep understanding that existed between these two there was no need for such an exchange of words.

And while Diane perhaps thought it queer that Jimmy Christopher should turn over the controls of the tank to Tim at such a crucial moment, and interest himself in an unimportant vial, she asked no questions. It was Jimmy Christopher, himself, who vouchsafed the explanation. "If Satterlee dies," he said, "he will never know what he has done for the country."

"W-what do you mean?" Marie Joyce asked.

Jimmy Christopher had to raise his voice now to be heard, for the sound of cannonading had increased to a crescendo of infernal madness. Enemy artillery was sending over high explosive shells in an endeavor to wipe out the little tank which was speeding northward across the plain under Tim Donovan's guidance. "Satterlee told me just before he lost consciousness that Major Horty tried to drink from this vial when he thought he was being infected with the plague!"

Jimmy's eyes met those of Diane in a long glance. "Do you know what that means?"

Diane nodded. "It must mean—that the vial contains—an antitoxin for the plague!"

Operator 5's lips tightened. "Di, we've *got* to escape from this artillery fire—not for our own sakes. If we can get this vial into a laboratory and analyze its contents, it may mean the salvation of the country from the plague!"

Diane's glance held high faith. Above the din of the deafening gunfire her voice came steady and courageous: "I think that God will guide us to safety. He would not have brought us this far otherwise."

For a moment there was a space of devout silence in the cramped quarters of that little tank. And then, throwing his shoulders back, Operator 5 strode resolutely forward to take the controls from Tim....

CHAPTER 7
TWO SLIM CHANCES

THE PURSUING enemy tanks had fallen behind, no doubt to leave a clear field for the Purple artillery. Now the enemy shells began coming over so thick and fast that the sun was obscured by the constant, unceasing bursts of fire and flame from the exploding enemy projectiles. While Diane and Marie Joyce ministered to the wounded, Jimmy drove grimly ahead, his eyes barely able to pierce through the fog of dust and flying earth in front of him.

The enemy tanks were no doubt giving the range to their big guns behind the lines, and now, as more and more batteries began concentrating their fire on this one fleeing baby tank, the earth seemed to be in a constant volcanic eruption all around them. A curtain of fire seemed to blot out the sky and the field ahead. Abruptly the whole body of the tank seemed to be jarred as a huge shell burst close alongside them. Coleman, one of the

Americans who had manned a gun in the tank, gripped Jimmy by the shoulder.

"God, Operator 5!" he exclaimed hoarsely, "we can't get through. They're laying down a curtain in front of us to cut off our escape!"

Jimmy Christopher said bitterly: "We can't go back, Coleman, so we have to go on."

He headed the tank directly into the fire-screen ahead of them. Suddenly Tim Donovan uttered a wild exclamation from the rear of the tank, where he had been puttering around with a radio set installed close beside the after guns. "Jimmy!" the lad shouted. "I've cut in on the enemy shortwave. The tanks behind us are talking to their headquarters, but I can't understand everything they're saying—"

Jimmy Christopher's face lighted with sudden inspiration. "Take the controls, Coleman!" he shouted, and fairly hurled himself across the short distance to where Tim stood at the radio. It was a combination sending and receiving set, and Tim watched with wide, excited eyes as Operator 5 fitted the headphones to his ears. Above the din of the terrific barrage that was being laid down across their path, Jimmy could hear the guttural voice of a tank commander speaking in the language of the Central Empire: "The range is about a hundred yards too long, Herr Colonel. But hold it as it is, they are blanketed in now and the American fools are driving directly toward your barrage curtain—"

Jimmy Christopher winked at Tim and manipulated the controls of the sending set, then barked into the microphone in an exact duplication of the tank commander's voice: *"Gott in Himmel, Herr Colonel!* The Yankees have turned around. They are coming back toward us. Drop your barrage two hundred yards—quickly!"

Almost instantaneously the dreadful drumfire of the barrage ceased. The sudden quiet, that was almost startling by contrast with the din of the bombardment, descended upon them. Jimmy covered the microphone with his hand and shouted: "Full speed ahead, Coleman!"

Coleman needed no second order. The little tank fairly flew through the air as it bounced over ruts and shell holes.

Operator 5, listening tensely with the earphones clamped to his ears, heard the Central Empire tank commander shouting frantically: "No, no, Herr Colonel—"

But Jimmy had already seized the microphone, dragged it over close to the after machine gun. He pulled the trip of the gun and the sharp, clattering staccato of its rapid-fire explosions sent a cacophony of sound through the microphone out over the ether. The voice of the tank commander was completely drowned out. And even as Jimmy watched through the rear porthole he saw the deadly barrage descend two hundred yards back, directly upon the five pursuing enemy tanks. The enemy artillery was shelling its own tank squadron!

Two direct hits were scored almost at once, and Jimmy Christopher's face was set in stern lines as he saw the two leading tanks practically smashed apart by the heavy projectiles. He got a glimpse of the three other tanks racing forward, and then a curtain of flame descended in front of those three monsters, as the whole power of the enemy barrage was laid down.

Operator 5 took his hand from the trip of the machine gun, and replaced the microphone. Tim Donovan was looking at him with admiration. "Gosh, Jimmy," the boy said in a hushed voice, "that was the slickest piece of work I ever saw you do!"

Jimmy patted the lad's shoulder, called out to Coleman urgently: "Change direction, Coleman. Drive straight west till you hit the Colorado. Ten minutes more and we'll be safe. By the time those tanks get their Herr Colonel to lift the barrage, we'll be out of sight—so they won't be able to give the artillery our range."

Now, as the little tank bumped across parched fields and deserted plains, the faces of those within it were alight with renewed hope. Not a soul there but had given up hope of living only a short while ago. Inoculated with the new, unknown, dreadful type of cholera virus, they had charged into enemy guns seeking only death; yet within a few minutes they saw themselves on the way to safety, saw themselves looking forward to a possible deliverance from the doom of cholera. No one doubted that the vial Jimmy Christopher had taken from Satterlee's pocket contained an antitoxin of some sort.

OPERATOR 5 let Coleman keep the controls, and himself went to the aid of Diane and Marie Joyce, who were ministering to the wounded. Satterlee was still unconscious, but his wounds had been cleaned, and he was resting more or less comfortably, with his head on his rolled-up uniform tunic. The wounded girls were being treated as fast as Diane and Marie could get to them. Tim Donovan was once again at the radio, trying to raise Z-7 in San Francisco.

Now the roar of the guns had subsided somewhat, as they moved farther and farther from the front. The pursuing enemy tanks did not appear behind them. Apparently they had either been destroyed by their own fire, or they realized they would have to penetrate too deep into American territory in order to catch up with the fugitives.

Tim Donovan, working with the earphones on his head, turned and called to Operator 5: "Jimmy! I've got Z-7! Come and talk to him!"

Jimmy Christopher took the phones from the boy, who added: "I've told him how we pulled out of that mess at the front. He wants you."

Jimmy said into the microphone: "Z-7! Operator 5 talking. We're headed west for the Colorado River. Pursuit left behind. What's new? Go ahead."

"Jimmy!" Z-7's voice came over the ether. "Tim told me that the serum is ineffective, because the cholera virus is not the usual type. We've just got word from other infected cities. It's the same thing. People are dying like flies, and the serum doesn't help. For God's sake, don't lose that vial. Get it analyzed as fast as you can. Every minute counts. Enemy planes have dropped more bacteria all along the front. If we don't develop an antitoxin our Defense Force will be decimated!"

"Okay, Z-7," Jimmy returned quietly. "We'll get this vial to a laboratory as quickly as possible. Send a plane to meet us at the

Colorado, where Highway 60 crosses the river. You can fly the stuff to San Francisco and I'll go on to San Diego with the tank."

He signed off, and turned to see Tim Donovan crowding against the forward turret porthole, alongside of Coleman, and looking out at something to the south. "Come here, Jimmy," Tim called. "Look at that plane. It seems to be in trouble. It doesn't look like a Central Empire plane—"

He pointed upward as Jimmy joined him. There, angling down toward a field directly ahead of them, was a huge, trimotored passenger plane. Thick plumes of black smoke were spilling from the rear, where its reserve tanks were located.

Even as they watched, the plane bounced to an awkward, hurried landing, and five figures leaped out, began running away. Two of those running figures were pilots, and the other three were brilliantly uniformed officers—but not in the uniforms of the Central Empire. Hardly had those fleeing men raced fifty feet away from the crippled plane than they saw the approaching tank and pulled up short.

Jimmy Christopher said to Coleman: "Pull up. Those are Mexican officers. Wonder what they're doing, flying northeast. If they were going to San Francisco to confer with Z-7 they wouldn't be this far over."

The tank rumbled to a stop, and Jimmy opened the porthole, peered out. The leading officer stopped and raised his hand, called out: "Our plane is burning. Thank God a Central Empire tank has found us. We were afraid that we would be captured by the Americans!"

Jimmy Christopher frowned. He noted that the American

flag that had been hoisted in the rear had been shot away, and that the only clue to the identity of the tank now was the insignia of the severed head and the crossed broadswords painted on the prow.

"Who are you?" he demanded of the man who had spoken.

"I am General Barrenos, and these are my aides. We are flying to Denver for a conference with Baron Flexner and His Imperial Majesty, the Emperor Rudolph. Can you give us transportation?"

Jimmy glanced backward at the others in the tank, who were listening tensely to the conversation. Since it was being conducted in Spanish, only Diane could understand. She raised her eyes to Jimmy.

"They—they're going to join the Central Empire—"

Jimmy stopped her, raising his hand for silence. The five Mexicans had approached quite close to the tank.

"We are afraid our ship will explode. Please take us in, and carry us to your Emperor—"

"What is your business with our Emperor?" Jimmy demanded gruffly. "You say you are General Barrenos. I know of no such name in the Mexican government—"

Barrenos, a stout, flabby-faced man, interrupted: "It is that I am the General Arnaldo Barrenos, who leads the revolution which will overthrow the present government in Mexico City. Your Emperor has promised to support the revolution, and I go to meet him and Baron Flexner."

Operator 5 felt a chill creep up his spine. If Rudolph was planning to finance a revolution in Mexico, it was a shrewd blow.

The present Mexican government was, of course, in sympathy with the United States, was even now raising an army to support the American Defense Force, was rounding up every available barrel of oil to ship to San Francisco. If the president were overthrown, if a puppet of Rudolph's, like Barrenos, were to attain power, then there was little hope for the United States.

The smoke was coming ever thicker from the huge plane, and the Mexican pilots watched it nervously. Diane left her patients and came to Operator 5's side in the tank. "Jimmy, what are you going to do? This man Barrenos is the instrument by which Rudolph plans to crush us—"

Jimmy Christopher nodded. "God seems to be on our side today—bringing Barrenos here this way!"

He swung open the turret and swiveled the forward machine gun around so that it pointed at the little group of Mexicans. "Gentlemen," he called out courteously, "I am sorry to inform you that you are very unfortunate. You have fallen into the hands of the wrong people. We are Americans!"

BARRENOS UTTERED an oath as he saw Jimmy, and the Mexicans turned to run. Jimmy fired off a short burst alongside them, and they stopped short, their hands in the air. "Take the gun, Coleman," Jimmy commanded, and himself climbed out of the tank. Barrenos and the other Mexicans watched him as he passed them, giving them a wide berth, so that Coleman could spray them with the gun if they attempted resistance. Barrenos' face was a study in rage and frustration, and Jimmy grinned at him cheerfully. "Don't take it too hard, General. It's the fortunes of war!"

He hurried over to the smoking plane and climbed into the passenger compartment. At once he found the source of the smoke. "As I thought," he muttered. The smoke was coming from the floorboards of the passenger compartment, and flames were beginning to beat up through the cracks. It was not as serious as it looked. The batteries for the interior lighting and ignition were stored here, and some crossed wires had caused a short circuit.

Jimmy ripped an extinguisher from the wall, and sprayed the burning spot. In a few moments the fire was entirely under control. The Mexicans might have done the same thing that Jimmy had done, but they had given way to panic at the first appearance of the smoke.

Jimmy chuckled as a plan began to form in his mind. He left the plane, went back to the tank, passing Barrenos and his group once more. The pilots glared at him, raging because they had failed to douse the fire themselves, and had thus put themselves in the hands of the Americans. According to the Latin-American code, revolutionaries are given short shrift, and these men expected only to be summarily shot.

But Jimmy let them suffer in their own terror for a while. He called Coleman and Graves out of the tank. "The battery in that plane is ruined by fire," he told them. "Do you think you could take the auxiliary lighting battery out of the tank and install it in the plane?"

Graves nodded with assurance. "I could do it, Operator 5. I used to run an automobile ignition store in Topeka before the Purple troops drove us out of there."

"Go to it," Jimmy told him. "And try to make a snappy job of it!"

Tim Donovan had taken over the machine gun, and while Coleman and Graves hastened over to the plane, Tim kept the gun trained on the five Mexican revolutionaries. Jimmy Christopher ordered them pleasantly to disarm, and they were compelled to drop their weapons in a small pile on the ground.

Then Operator 5 addressed their leader: "General Barrenos, I must now ask you a few questions. First, I wish to know whether you or any of these gentlemen with you have ever met any of Emperor Rudolph's staff. Second—who invited you to this conference at Denver? Third—what manner of identification do you carry with you, and fourth, whether you or any of these gentlemen in your group speaks the language of the Central Empire?"

Barrenos grinned thinly, showing two rows of even white teeth. "I shall answer nothing, señor. We Mexicans are not afraid to die. Tell your man to spray us with his machine gun—"

Jimmy Christopher held up a hand, said courteously: "I have always admired the courage of our neighbors in the Republic of Mexico. I do not doubt that you are ready to die by machine-gun bullets. I have, therefore, devised a different alternative for you if you refuse to answer."

Barrenos and the others stared at each other uneasily. Finally Barrenos shrugged. "I did not know that you Americans tortured prisoners—"

"Not at all," Jimmy assured him. "I will demonstrate to you what I intend." He raised his voice. "Di! Come out here, please."

In a moment Diane Elliot had climbed out of the tank, and stood next to Jimmy. "Will you be good enough to tell these gentlemen, in Spanish, what happened in Phoenix before I arrived?"

Diane glanced from Operator 5 to Barrenos and his aides, then spoke slowly. "We were holding the town against the enemy barrage, until they sent over a plane that dropped cholera germs. Everybody in the town became infected. Rather than die by the plague, we charged the enemy lines. Barely a dozen of us survived, but we are all inoculated with Asiatic Plague."

The Mexicans grew pale as she uttered the word. It was remarkable how brave men, who were not afraid to face death in battle, blanched at the thought of contracting the plague.

Jimmy pressed his advantage. "Furthermore," he told them, "we have found that it is a type of Asiatic cholera that is unknown in the west, and one which cannot be cured by any antitoxin now known to us. You understand, therefore, that to contract the disease is certain death."

Barrenos asked uneasily: "B-but what has this to do with—us?"

"Just this," Jimmy Christopher told him grimly. "If you refuse to answer my questions, and to comply with the simple request that I shall presently make, you will be taken into the tank with us. You will contract the plague. On the other hand, if you do what I ask, you will be allowed to go free."

There was a shrewd glint in the eyes of the Mexican general. "How do I know, señor, that you and this young lady speak the truth? Perhaps you merely invent this horrible plague—"

Jimmy motioned impatiently. "If you will step into the tank you will see the proof of our words. Miss Elliot and myself arrived in Phoenix only a few hours ago, and so the plague has not developed in us. But inside the tank are several persons who are dying of the cholera. Look for yourself!"

Barrenos glanced at his companions, then stepped timidly to the tank, and peered in through the open turret. He plainly saw the rows of patients, saw their agony. He turned away in revulsion, careful not to touch any part of the tank, and not to approach too near Diane or Jimmy. Diane threw him a sardonic glance, and went back into the tank.

Barrenos returned to his companions, shoulders drooping, and whispered with them for a moment; then he faced Jimmy. "You—you have won, señor. We will do—whatever you ask!

"Good!" Jimmy exclaimed. "Now for my questions. Which of you are personally acquainted with Rudolph or any of his staff?"

"None of us, señor. We were invited to the conference by cable from Denver. As for identification, I carry this commission from the Provisional Government of the Mexican Revolutionary Army—" he withdrew a long envelope and tossed it to Jimmy—"which carries my appointment as generalissimo of the rebel forces, and empowers me to make treaties with the Central Empire."

JIMMY PICKED up the commission and examined it. "Do you or any of your companions speak the language of the Central Empire?

"I speak it, señor," Barrenos told him. "None of my associates understand it, however."

While this had been going on, Coleman and Graves had made several trips back and forth from the plane to the tank. Now the plane's motors stuttered to life as Graves turned them over. Then he and Coleman came running to Jimmy. "We've got it fixed, Operator 5!" Graves exclaimed triumphantly. "She's as good as new!"

Jimmy nodded. "And now, gentlemen," he informed the Mexicans, "I have only one more request to make. We must have three of your uniforms—yours, General Barrenos, that of one of your aides and of one of your pilots. Since you all have greatcoats, you three gentlemen can cover yourselves with them. You will then march ahead of the tank as far as the Colorado River, where an American plane will meet you. You will be held for forty-eight hours, to give me time to execute a plan of my own and then you will be freed in accordance with my promise."

The Mexicans began a tumultuous argument. It would be an affront to their honor to have their uniforms taken from them. They would rather die than submit to such an indignity.

To all their protestations Jimmy Christopher listened unyieldingly. In the end they were forced to obey. Jimmy ordered Graves to don the pilot's uniform, and Coleman put on the clothes of the aide. He himself got into the bright uniform of General Arnaldo Barrenos. The Mexicans did not avail themselves of Jimmy's offer of his own clothes and those of Graves and Coleman in exchange for their own, because they wouldn't touch anything that might carry the plague germs. Instead they covered themselves with overcoats and waited moodily while

Jimmy Christopher conferred with Tim Donovan and Diane, inside the tank.

"Escort these men to the Colorado and turn them over to the plane that Z-7 is sending. Here's the vial, Di, that I took from Satterlee's pocket. You know what to do with it."

Diane nodded somberly. They were all watching each other furtively now for signs of the breaking out of the cholera. Those in the tank were suffering from it violently, and it would only be a matter of hours before they, too, would be struck down by it. In the meantime, however, they were going ahead courageously with what they had to do, ignoring the deadly menace of the plague that they knew was coursing through their bloodstreams.

"I'll have the few drops in this vial analyzed," Diane said, "and then they can start manufacture of it on a large scale. If it turns out to be the proper antitoxin for the plague, we can rush it to all infected areas."

While he talked, Operator 5 had taken from a pocket a flat, compact, folding case, which, when opened, revealed orderly rows of makeup tubes, pigment and plastic material. The inside cover of the case was a mirror, and Jimmy let Diane hold it up while he worked swiftly with the contents of the case. Soon Jimmy's face began to lose its characteristic features under his deft manipulation. It became flabby in appearance, his jaws seemed to become thicker, and his nostrils wider. His skin assumed a swarthy complexion. In a few moments he had become the personification of a Mexican general.

In turn he called in Graves and Coleman, added a few touches to their appearance, so that the three of them would have passed anywhere for Mexicans.

Tim Donovan, watching him intently, said: "Looks like you're planning a little jaunt to Denver, Jimmy. How about taking me?"

There was a strange wistfulness in the boy's voice. He had accompanied Operator 5 almost everywhere of late, and the two had been through much together. Now the lad knew that they might never see each other again. Instinctively he felt that Operator 5 had no great hope of a serum being developed from the small quantity of the specimen in the vial, and that he was staking everything in a desperate attempt to contact Nan in Denver and discover the secret of the plague at first hand. Tim also felt the cholera would overtake himself, Diane and Jimmy long before they could penetrate its secret; and he wanted Operator 5 to be with them when they died.

Jimmy Christopher looked at the boy affectionately. Between them there was no need of lengthy speeches. He understood the boy's mood. But he shook his head regretfully, spoke with an attempt at banter: "Sorry, Tim, but I haven't got any dwarf or gnome clothes for you—and that's all you could pass as. I guess you'll have to stay with Diane. Anyway, someone is needed to drive the tank and keep a watch on our Mexican friends."

He shook hands solemnly with Tim, and then stepped aside with Diane for a moment. In her eyes there was a slight suspicion of wetness. "Jimmy!" she murmured. "Back there at Phoenix, I was ready to die. I had resigned myself to leaving you that way. And then you showed up, and all my hopes revived again.

Now—" her voice choked a bit—"I—find it hard to think of—dying alone. Must you go?"

He nodded. "I'm afraid we're all doomed—Tim and you and I, and these others. We've got the plague in our blood, and there's no use dodging the fact. It's only a matter of hours before it gets us. There are only two slim chances—your work in the lab in San Diego, and my work in Denver. But if we both fail, then it's—good-bye, Di!"

Diane Elliot uttered a low sob, and impulsively threw herself into his arms. Jimmy Christopher enfolded her slim body, pressed her close to him. His lips brushed her soft chestnut hair. He held her that way a moment, feeling the life and vitality of her. The yearning of her whole body beat against his breast; then he pushed her away almost gruffly, and walked without looking back, toward the waiting plane.

In a few moments they had taken off, and were leaving the tank far behind, down below. Glancing back over his shoulder, Jimmy could still see the tense figure of Diane Elliot standing down there, looking up....

CHAPTER 8
THE SILVER STATUE

HIS IMPERIAL MAJESTY, Rudolph I, Lord of the Central Empire, Emperor of Europe and Asia, Conqueror of America, was in a mildly genial mood.

In the basement of the Denver Mint Building he was surveying the preparations for a unique ceremony. Accompanied by

Baron Flexner and a few chosen courtiers, he was standing before a small blast furnace. The heat from the hearth of this furnace was terrific, and threw a ruddy glow upon the faces of all those present. A white-coated engineer, upon whose sleeve was embroidered the symbol of the severed head and the crossed broadswords, was deferentially whispering in the Emperor's ear.

"We are raising the temperature of the silver, Your Majesty, to 1762 degrees Fahrenheit, which is its melting point. As soon as the preparations are complete, the silver will be placed in the furnace under hot blast, and will be poured in molten state into the vat—"

"I understand, Rador," Rudolph interrupted impatiently. "How soon will the silver be ready to pour?"

"In a half hour, Your Majesty."

"Very well." The Emperor motioned to one of his courtiers. "Instruct Captain Meister to bring down the Christopher girl!"

The courtier bowed, and backed out. Rudolph's features were twisted into the sadistic smile his courtiers had grown to know and dread. He rubbed his hands with satisfaction. "You see, Flexner, what I have devised? The Christopher girl will be very sorry that she gave herself up—very, very sorry!"

Flexner stirred nervously, and threw a swift glance at a dark young woman who stood at Rudolph's left. This woman was dressed in a long white dress that trailed the floor, but clung tightly to her voluptuous figure. Upon her shoulders was a short ermine cape, rivaled in whiteness only by her throat and bosom. The fiery heat from the blast furnace only served to accentuate the passionate fire that dwelt in her eyes. Flexner said uneasily: "Perhaps the Baroness Anita will not care to witness the sight—"

Rudolph laughed. "Anita doesn't mind." He stroked the woman's arm. "In fact, she delights in these things. Don't you, Anita?"

The Baroness Anita Monfred,* cousin of Rudolph, shuddered slightly, and a barely perceptible grimace of revulsion passed over her beautiful countenance. "I—don't quite understand what you're—going to do with this molten silver, Rudolph," she said.

He rubbed his hands in gleeful anticipation. "I'm going to

---

* AUTHOR'S NOTE: Those who are familiar with the history of the early days of the Purple Invasion will recall the Baroness Anita Monfred, who was several times instrumental in serving Operator 5—in spite of the fact that she was Rudolph's cousin. In her blood there coursed the same peculiar, wildly passionate, cruel nature of Rudolph, together with a gentle compassion inherited from her mother. At times she was capable of pantherish rage and cruelty; at others, of an unexplainable tenderness. She was an enigma to herself as well as to Rudolph, who hoped some time to make her the empress of the world. And if she was herself capable of dreadful rages, she was more less of a leavening influence of Rudolph. Unfortunately, she had experienced an attraction toward Operator 5 when she had first met him in the first wave of the Purple Invasion. She had virtually offered herself to him, only to be met with coldness, and her hate for Jimmy Christopher now equaled the passion she had once felt for him. Nevertheless she still viewed with revulsion many of her cousin's excesses of inhuman cruelty.

erect a statue in front of the Mint Building, Anita," he told her. "A statue of silver. A beautiful, tall column of pure silver!"

He pointed to a vat some ten feet in length and three feet wide lying at the mouth of the blast furnace. "The silver is going to be poured into that vat to form the monument.

"But—" Anita's puzzled glance studied the vat—"I don't see what that has to do with the Christopher girl. Why do you order Operator 5's sister to be brought down here?"

"Patience, dear Anita, and you shall see!"

The Emperor turned to Flexner, who had just been handed a dispatch by an orderly. "Good news, or bad, Baron?"

Flexner read it, and his sallow face flushed, so that it was hard to tell whether the glow in his cheeks was due to emotion or to the blasts of hot air from the furnace. "It is from the front, Sire, from the Phoenix sector. Marshal Kremer's plan to drive the plague-ridden defenders into the American back country has failed. They refused to accept the armistice he offered them, and charged our trenches. All but a scant half-dozen died under our guns. That half-dozen was rescued by—Operator 5. He must have seized one of our tanks. He carried off the survivors. It is thought that he also found a vial of our anti-cholera serum on one of our own officers!"

Rudolph's eyes blazed with dreadful fury. "That man! That Operator 5! Always he balks me! Is one man to laugh at all my armies? Can none of you catch him for me?" He swung in murderous rage upon his courtiers and they shrank from him. "Are you all impotent? Am I surrounded by idiots? Why doesn't one of you think of a plan to capture him?"

Flexner stammered: "Sire, it—it is my dearest wish to capture that man. But give me time—"

"Time! Time! That's all you can think of! In the meanwhile he upsets my best plans, mocks me! I—"

His frenzied outburst resulted in a fit of coughing, and Anita Monfred put a white hand on his arm. "Don't excite yourself, cousin. Why give way to your anger? Operator 5 will only laugh at you the more. Be patient. Surely he will do something soon that will bring him into our power, just as his sister is now—"

She paused as a file of troopers marched into the room, led by a stout Central Empire captain. Between the double file of guards marched Nan Christopher!

SHE HELD her head high, and walked with shoulders back. Her hands were tied behind her back. The troopers halted and the captain saluted, said: "Your Imperial Majesty, Captain Meister reports with the prisoner, Nan Christopher!"

Rudolph smiled sourly. He had not yet recovered from his rage. His small, mean eyes studied the slim loveliness of Nan. "Yes, yes," he muttered. "She looks just like that brother of hers. I shall watch her agony, and think it is Operator 5 whom I see squirm!"

He took a step toward her, and spat out: "Well? Have you decided to tell us where your accomplices are hidden? We have searched the entire Union Hotel, but we cannot find them. Manifestly, they must be hidden somewhere in the hotel, for you came out of it. Speak. Tell us where they hide, or the next half hour of your life will be your last—and the most frightful!"

Nan forced a brave smile. Her eyes took in the blast furnace, the empty vat, and she restrained a shudder. In a cool, clear voice, she said: "I have nothing to tell you, Rudolph, except that you are a vile beast. Now please go ahead with your—performance!"

Flexner and the Baroness Anita Monfred threw her grudging glances of admiration. But Rudolph snarled: "We shall hear you beg for mercy yet!"

He gestured angrily, and the troopers seized her under the direction of the engineer, Rador, and laid her in the empty vat. She lay very still, on her back, staring up unblinkingly at Rudolph and the others who watched her from above. Rudolph said gloatingly: "Perhaps you understand what I am about to do with you?"

Nan didn't answer, and he went on. "You doubtless know that this is a blast furnace for melting silver. I am having a monument cast, to be erected outside this building. It will be a grand monument, and it will be of particular significance to your brother. For inside of this statue will repose *the body of his sister!* Yes—" as he heard a gasp from Anita Monfred—"I am having Miss Christopher cast in silver. The molten metal will be poured into the vat around her living body!"

In her coffinlike vat Nan Christopher stiffened. Her eyes suddenly widened, but by no other sign did she indicate that she had heard what was to be done to her. Involuntarily, however, her glance rose to the insulated sleeve that ran from the blast furnace down to the vat. It was through that tube that the molten silver would roll to sizzle around her body!

Anita Monfred exclaimed: "Rudolph! You can't do such a thing—"

He laughed. "Can't I? Rador! Is the silver ready?

"In ten minutes, Your Majesty!"

Anita Monfred stepped close to the edge of the vat, stretched out her hands appealingly to Nan. "In God's name, speak! Tell him where your friends are hidden. Surely, they would not want you to meet such a fate in order to protect them. No woman can be expected to allow herself to be buried in hot silver. In God's name, *speak!*"

Slowly, Nan shook her head. The taut lines of her face now indicated the strain she was laboring under. She was silent, for she did not trust herself to speak. But her eyes glowed defiantly.

Anita turned away from the vat with drooping shoulders. Her lowered glance refused to meet that of Rudolph. "My cousin," she murmured, "though I hate Operator 5, I hate you much more at this moment. The girl is right. You are a vile beast!"

Rudolph only laughed. He was rubbing his hands, his eyes shining with an unholy joy. He licked his thick lips just as a beast might do in anticipation of a kill....

SOME TWENTY feet below the spot where Rudolph was standing, below the foundation pillars of the building, ten sweating, toiling men were working desperately, frenziedly, to break through the concrete side of the elevator shaft. Had Rudolph and the others paused to listen carefully, they might have caught the dull sound of pickaxe blows. But MacTavish, Slips McGuire and the others had encountered an obstacle that neither they nor John Carrone, the original digger of the tunnel, had foreseen.

The concrete shaft had been threaded with thick meshed wire which made it terribly difficult to cut through. Though the filed plans of the Mint Building had disclosed the fact that the elevator shaft went down below the foundation level itself, they had not disclosed the fact that the architects had recognized the weak spot, and had guarded against it by inserting the wire mesh. In addition to this, one series of wires in that mesh had been electrified. Disturbing this series would ordinarily have set off an alarm in the building; but the Purple Invaders had failed to connect the system, so that the tunnelers still remained undiscovered.

Nevertheless, the job would take days instead of hours. And MacTavish and McGuire labored frantically as they realized that Nan must be undergoing a mental inquisition wondering about their whereabouts—and their progress.

They had seriously discussed the question of going up and surrendering themselves, but this had been voted down for the time being. They still hoped to be able to break through the shaft. So they swung pickaxes, and dug frenziedly with hammer and chisel, while above them Nan lay in the coffinlike vat, waiting for the silver to be converted into a molten stream to inundate her body.

AS SHE lay there, looking defiantly up at the almost brute-like face of the man who was military master of more than half the world, she seemed to be a modern Joan of Arc, offering herself up as a sacrifice for a country she loved more than life itself. Rador, the engineer, standing near the lever which would release the molten silver to pour down upon her, leered across the room at Rudolph, turning every few moments to peer at a temperature gauge.

"In a few moments, Your Majesty," he said.

Anita Monfred was standing taut, a hand pressed hard against her breast, unable to take her eyes from the face of Nan Christopher. Flexner stood close beside Rudolph, his eyes also glued to the countenance of the young woman who was about to be martyred. The half-dozen courtiers watched silently, shifting uneasily from one foot to the other. Though by their natures they could find it in themselves to enjoy such a sight thoroughly, there was none of them whose pleasure was not soured by the thought that he himself might be the next to be placed in the vat.

So variable was Rudolph's whim, so uncontrolled his anger, that he might at any moment order one of these to be executed next.

And so, in the terrific heat exuded by the furnace, that tableau was almost motionless; while outside, all over the country, great guns thundered, and men fought and died, and a nation was slowly being ground under the heel of a merciless conqueror. Cholera raged in cities and in trenches, and upstairs in this very building, nervous chemists played with retorts and with germs, and bred deadly bacteria.

Rador's eyes were fixed on the gauge. The heat had become almost unbearable. The needle of the gauge was hovering near the 1700 mark on the Fahrenheit scale.

"Well, Rador, are you ready?"

"In another moment, Majesty. But a few degrees more, and it is done!"

Rudolph smirked at Nan, who still gazed up at him defiantly. "Perhaps you will speak now? If you will betray your accomplices

123

to me, I promise to spare you this particular form of death. I shall substitute them instead of you. Come! Speak up!"

Nan gulped. In the vat, the heat was even more intense than where the others stood. The outlet of the funnel leading from the furnace was only a few inches from her side. When Rador depressed that lever, hot molten silver would come oozing out of that funnel to roll slowly toward her, to encompass her in its slimy folds. Long before it entirely covered her, she would, of course, be dead. But she anticipated in her imagination, a thousand times, the agony she would undergo before merciful death would finally yield her oblivion. Yet she managed to smile saucily.

"If I weren't a lady, Your Imperial Majesty," she said, "I would tell you to go to hell!"

CHAPTER 9
RECOGNITION!

WHEN OPERATOR 5 landed the big trimotored plane at the airport just outside of Denver, he was met by an imperial staff car which had evidently been expecting the arrival of the Mexican delegation. Jimmy carried himself with just the amount of swagger that General Barrenos might have affected. But Coleman, dressed in the uniform of a Mexican major, was nervous, as was Graves, who wore the clothes of the pilot.

As Jimmy brought the plane to a perfect landing on the field, he said to them: "Keep a stiff upper lip, boys, and don't talk.

124

Neither of you can speak Spanish, so it'll be ticklish for a while. If you're spoken to, act as if you were chewing on the answer, and I'll jump into the breach and reply for you. Then you smile as if I'd just taken the words out of your mouth, and say, '*Segura, señor!*' Get it?"

Coleman nodded, practiced the words. "*Segura,* señor! I get it all right."

Graves repeated the words, too. "I hope we get by, Operator 5. Won't those guys get suspicious?"

Jimmy grinned. "You don't know court etiquette. The Emperor won't even notice low guys like you. And the others won't get a chance to talk to you—if I can help it! Anyway, we've got to take that chance. It would look awful queer for General Barrenos to come here alone." His voice dropped as they made ready to descend from the plane. "Look sharp, now! Here comes the reception committee!"

The imperial staff car had pulled up close to the plane, and a portly officer got out, bowed low. "General Barrenos, I presume? Permit me to introduce myself. I am Colonel Humbert Strohmer, of the personal staff of his Imperial Majesty, Emperor Rudolph I. I see that you have arrived on schedule."

Jimmy returned Colonel Strohmer's bow. "We had a very pleasant trip. These—" he indicated Coleman and Graves—"are my two aides, Major Colamanni, and Lieutenant Gravés!"

Strohmer gave them only a cursory greeting, and it was fortunate that he did not pay them more attention, for Coleman and Graves were finding it difficult to restrain the burst of laughter that welled to their lips at the sudden Latinization of their names.

Strohmer led them to the staff car, ordered the chauffeur: "Back to Imperial Headquarters, Carl!"

As the powerful car roared back toward Denver, Strohmer turned courteously to Jimmy. "His Majesty ordered me to bring you directly into his presence the moment you arrived. It appears that he wishes to come to an understanding with you at once."

"That is good," Jimmy returned. "Mexico is ripe for revolution. With the proper backing, I can gain control in a week."

He had already entered entirely into the spirit of the man whose identity he had stolen, and he was speaking—and even thinking—just as Barrenos would have.

When the car arrived in front of the Mint Building, the company of Imperial Hussars presented arms sharply, and stood at attention. Jimmy smiled at the thought of how these Imperial Hussars and their commanding officer would feel if they knew they were saluting the man whom their Emperor hated most in the world. But he was more interested in the Union Hotel, across the street. His eyes narrowed as he noted the cordon of soldiers around the old building.

Colonel Strohmer had already gotten out of the staff car, and Jimmy descended, asked casually: "What are those soldiers doing around that old building? It would seem that there is a personage of some importance in there."

Strohmer laughed. "That is very funny, General Barrenos. We learned this morning that the sister of Operator 5 was hiding there, with some companions. But search as we would, we could not find them. Our Emperor was so eager to capture her, that he ordered the building dynamited, when—lo, she suddenly appeared, as if by magic. But her companions we cannot find. The emperor is—er—questioning the girl even now. I imagine he has devised some interesting method of questioning her!"

Jimmy felt suddenly cold inside. He saw Coleman and Graves exchange quick, startled glances. This news struck him like a body blow. He had come here expressly for the purpose of contacting Nan. Now he learned that she was a prisoner. No flicker of interest showed in his face as he asked slowly: "This girl—the sister of Operator 5—you say she is a prisoner? They have her in some prison?"

"No, no. She is being held right here in this building. The emperor wished to deal with her personally. I heard him say that he had a very clever idea for amusing her—something about a monument of silver."

"Let us go in," Jimmy said suddenly. "We must not keep the Emperor waiting!"

Strohmer bowed, and led the way past the Imperial Guards into the Mint Building. Coleman and Graves followed, nervously fingering the revolvers in their holsters.

A sergeant informed them that Rudolph was in the basement, and they descended, to be stopped by a guard outside the furnace room. Strohmer sent the guard in to announce them, and turned to Jimmy, saying apologetically: "You will forgive me, General Barrenos, but no strangers are permitted to enter the Emperor's presence armed. It will be necessary to relieve you of all weapons. You understand that I am only obeying orders—"

Operator 5 bowed. "Proceed, Colonel. I understand perfectly."
STROHMER WENT through their persons thoroughly,
removed the revolvers from their holsters, and took a small
.25 from Graves' inside pocket. He wagged a finger at Graves.
"These toy pistols are not much good, Lieutenant Gravés. You
should carry heavier firearms."

He spoke in the language of the Central Empire, and Graves
looked blank. Jimmy hastened to reply for him: "The lieutenant
always carries that small pistol with him, since he won it in a
lottery at Tiajuana. It is a memento to him."

Strohmer laughed. "That is different. Of course, it shall be
returned to you when you leave. You are satisfied?"

Jimmy said quickly: "Certainly he is!" And Graves smiled
blankly, suddenly remembered his cue and blurted: *"Segura,*
señor!" Then he looked at Jimmy as if for approval.

At that moment the guard came out and told them that the
Emperor would receive them at once. Strohmer led them into
the room where Rudolph stood above the vat, in front of the
blast furnace. Jimmy Christopher's quick glance took in the
whole room. He bowed to Rudolph, then straightened, nodding
to Flexner. Once more he bowed, very low, to the Baroness Anita
Monfred.

He had seen Nan in the vat the moment he put his foot inside
the door. But by no movement of face or body did he betray
more than an ordinary curiosity in the sight. He comprehended
the situation at once—the hot blast furnace, the pallid-featured
engineer, Rador, at the lever, the insulated tube through which
the molten silver would flow to envelope Nan's body. He saw

that his sister lay on her back, with hands bound, staring up at him and the others. There was as yet no recognition in her eyes. She did not know her brother under the greasy makeup of General Arnaldo Barrenos, the Mexican revolutionary.

The Emperor had at first frowned at the interruption, for Rador was on the point of announcing that the silver was ready; but when he learned that it was Barrenos, he had smiled and ordered the general admitted at once. Now he nodded graciously, and waved to Jimmy, who was prevented from approaching any closer by two of the courtiers, who motioned him back. It was an unbroken rule in the Emperor's household that no visitor—no matter how important—could approach closer than ten feet to His Imperial Highness. However, Rudolph was just now excessively friendly. Perhaps he welcomed this opportunity of exhibiting his clever, sadistic idea to the Mexican envoy.

"Welcome, General Barrenos!" he cried. "You have come just in time to witness a ceremony. That woman in the vat is the sister of Operator 5. I am going to erect a silver monument to her—and she shall be fittingly entombed in the monument. Clever, is it not?"

Jimmy Christopher restrained himself with difficulty. He managed a smile, and barely controlled his voice as he answered: "You are going to pour the molten silver over the girl, Your Majesty?

"That is what I intend to do, Barrenos. You have divined my idea. Barrenos, you are a clever man—a man after my own heart. We shall get along well. Now watch!" He turned to raise his hand in signal to Rador, and Nan Christopher's eyes opened wide as the dreaded moment arrived. In another instant she would be laved in the hot metal. Flexner watched her avidly, seeking in her face some trace of fear. The baron was a connoisseur of human pain and suffering, and he was enjoying this scene as much as his master.

The only one who did not enjoy it was Jimmy Christopher—and, perhaps, Anita Monfred. The Baroness Anita was dividing her attention between Nan and Operator 5. Her woman's eye had perceived something familiar about the way Jimmy walked, about the way he held his head. And she had been studying his face from the moment he entered. Now she watched both Jimmy and Nan. And she caught the tenseness of Operator 5, caught the desperate look of his eyes. Jimmy was about to spring into action. All the signs were there, the tautness of his body, poised as he was on his toes, with his elbows just a trifle away from his sides.

There were more than a dozen of Rudolph's men here, fully armed. Jimmy, Coleman and Graves had no guns at all; yet Jimmy Christopher would fight—that was certain.

And suddenly, in the flash of an eye, the Baroness Anita Monfred knew that General Barrenos was not General Barrenos, but Operator 5. She did not herself know what made her so sure. But her breasts heaved with sudden emotion, and all the hate that she felt for him suddenly welled up within her. Strangely, that hate was mingled with some other emotion that she could not identify. She had loved this man when she first saw him; perhaps she still loved him. If she did, however, she knew that she wanted to humiliate him, to conquer him, but *not kill him*.

And her woman's mind, leaping by instinct from thought to thought, moved her to interfere in this taut scene. Now, as Rudolph was about to raise his hand in signal, and as Jimmy was poised for precipitate, deadly action, Anita Monfred suddenly exclaimed in a high, sharp voice: "Wait, Rudolph!"

THE EMPEROR held the signal, looked at her darkly.

She stepped quickly forward, put a hand on his shoulder. "Rudolph, grant me a favor—"

"No!" he snapped. "You want me to spare the girl—"

"No, no. All I ask is that you delay her death for five minutes. I—there is something I wish to tell General Barrenos—in private—before that girl is embalmed in the silver. Grant me this whim, Rudolph!"

The Emperor frowned, puzzledly. "Anita, you are mad! You ask me to wait five minutes while you talk to Barrenos. You can have nothing to say to him. You have never seen him before. And what has it to do, anyway, with this—"

Anita moved very close to him, so that the perfume she used floated to his nostrils. Her soft body leaned against his for a moment, and she smiled up at him with full, red lips. "It is a strange request, Rudolph, but then you know that I do strange things. Grant me this, cousin—"

Baron Flexner, who stood on Rudolph's other side, broke in suavely: "Best be careful, Your Majesty. Remember, the Baroness Monfred wished you to spare the girl—"

It was perhaps Flexner's interference which caused the Emperor to accede to Anita's wish. He disliked being steered by Flexner, and often did just the opposite of what the baron recommended, merely to spite the man. Now he barked: "Quiet, Flexner! Do you dare to tell *me* what I shall or shall not do? You presume too far, my dear Baron. One day I shall grow impatient of you!"

He turned back to Anita, and nodded curtly. "You will have to explain to me later what you mean by all this folderol. But you may have your five minutes. Go talk to Barrenos!" He swung his dark scowl suspiciously toward Jimmy, then motioned to the engineer at the lever. "Wait, Rador!"

Anita threw the Emperor a grateful smile, and moved slowly across toward Jimmy Christopher. She drew him off into a corner where none could hear what they said, and stood facing him with her back to the others. She looked up into his face and spoke tauntingly, so low that he had to stoop to hear her whisper: "It is strange, General Barrenos, that you should be so interested in the sister of Operator 5!"

Jimmy met her gaze, and suddenly he understood that there was no use of pretense with this woman. She had pierced his disguise. She knew he was Operator 5.

He said in measured voice, dropping the accent he had used: "What is it you want of me, Baroness Anita? Since you know who I am, why do you not denounce me?"

Her black eyes bored into his. "Operator 5, you are the only man in the world whom I ever loved. Once I would have given up my position, everything; I would have followed you to the ends of the earth if you had but said the word. Now—I hate you!"

Jimmy glanced around at the roomful of men, all watching them intently, curiously; then at Nan, lying in the vat, staring up at him with suddenly wondering recognition. He nodded to her imperceptibly over Anita's shoulder, and saw the glad look came into her face, only to be swiftly replaced by one of absolute blankness as Nan Christopher sought to hide from the others her recognition of her brother.

The baroness was going on, talking very low, very swiftly. "Operator 5, what would you do to save your sister?"

Jimmy's eyes suddenly flickered with hope. "Anything!" he said.

"If I were to help you to save her, would you swear to cause your country's defenders to surrender to the Emperor?"

Jimmy Christopher's mouth tightened. "God help me, *no!*" he answered.

"I thought not. Would you exchange your own life for hers?"

"Yes."

"I will promise to help you to rescue your sister from that vat—on one condition."

"Name it."

"That after you have taken her to safety, you will return here and give yourself up—to me!"

Without hesitation Jimmy Christopher snapped: "I promise. I give you my word that I will return and surrender."

She nodded, her eyes suddenly gleaming. "Then be ready. I will take Rudolph out on some pretext. Then make your attempt. I will return and help you!"

Abruptly she swung away from him, smiling. Jauntily she walked over to Rudolph, who was glowering at her. She came close to the Emperor, whispered: "Rudolph! Come into the next

Jimmy's fist thudded into Rador's jaw—

room with me. There is something I must tell you!" She took him by the arm, and led him toward the side door, which opened into a smaller room off the furnace chamber.

Rudolph held back. "What is this madness, Anita? If you have anything to say—"

"Rudolph, I have just discovered something that is a matter of life or death. Quick, I warn you, if you remain here another moment, your life will be in danger!" As she spoke she threw a significant glance in the direction of Baron Flexner. Rudolph, like all other absolute monarchs, lived always in the shadow of the fear of assassination. Even Flexner was not above suspicion. And, like other despots who delighted in inflicting death and torture, he was innately a coward. Nothing could have appealed to him more strongly than the hint that there was immediate danger for him. He knew very well that Anita Monfred had more than once risked her own life for him. He knew that whatever her faults, she was blindly loyal to him as the head of her house. So he permitted himself to be led out of the chamber, into the next room.

This had originally been a storeroom for silver bars, and it was equipped with a double row of vaults and a corridor in the middle. These vaults were empty now, and had been converted by Rudolph into cells for those who displeased him. Now, the vault doors hung idly open, the empty cubicles attesting to the rape of their contents by the conquerors.

Just inside that room, Anita swung shut the door connecting to the furnace chamber. Rudolph frowned at her. "Quickly, Anita. What is it—"

"Just this, cousin dear," she told him sweetly. "That man who is posing as General Barrenos is not General Barrenos. He is Operator 5. In another moment he would have made a desperate attempt to rescue his sister, and I have no doubt that he would also have attempted your life. So I decided to take things into my own hands. You will be safe here for a while!"

And suddenly she placed both hands on his chest, and shoved hard.

TAKEN UNAWARES, he stumbled backward, shouting for help. But he lost his balance, tumbled into the nearest vault, his voice re-echoing through the room. Before he could regain his feet, Anita had slammed shut the vault door, and slipped home the huge steel bolt. Then, breathless from her swift exertion, she ran to the other end of the room, where a stand of rifles was stacked near the far door. She snatched up one, made sure that it was loaded, and raced swiftly back toward the furnace room.

All this had taken a scant two minutes. Jimmy Christopher, back in the furnace chamber, had not quite understood the motives behind Anita Monfred's strange actions. But he seized at her offer of help—even if it was granted at the price of his own life.

He tensed as the door closed behind Anita and Rudolph, and threw a warning glance at Coleman and Graves. And it was at that moment that Rudolph's cry for help came to them from the next room. Flexner and the courtiers were stung into immobility by their Emperor's call for aid. But Rador's reaction was different. Almost instinctively, his hand pressed against the lever that would release the flow of liquid silver.

And in that instant Jimmy Christopher leaped across the intervening space at Rador. The lever was halfway down when Jimmy's fist thudded into the engineer's jaw. Rador went backwards, and his head smashed against the wall with a nasty thud. Jimmy himself reached for the lever to yank it up again, but by that time Flexner had grasped the situation. "Stop him!" he shrieked, and flung himself at Operator 5. His clutching fingers caught at Jimmy's tunic and dragged him away from the lever. Half a dozen of the courtiers leaped to aid Flexner, and Coleman and Graves threw themselves headlong in the path of those courtiers, battling them with their fists.

Jimmy Christopher strove frantically to thrust through the mass of men who had suddenly leaped at him, and who were now between him and the lever. He threw a frantic glance toward the vat, saw with horrified eyes that the white-hot metal had already trickled into the compartment, and was slowly oozing toward Nan's body. Nan squirmed away from it, tried to raise herself to a sitting position, but she was hampered by the bonds that held her hands behind her. And every motion she made brought her nearer to the greedy heat of the slowly flowing silver.

Fists thudded into bodies, men groaned and cursed. Jimmy Christopher's bunched fists moved in and out swiftly with the continuous motion of pistons. But the odds were too great. Coleman and Graves were snowed under, and several of the courtiers not in the press about Jimmy had drawn guns and were coolly waiting for a chance to shoot him down.

Nan cried from where she lay in the vat: "Run, Jimmy! Never mind me! Get away—"

A shot drowned out her voice, and a slug whined close to Jimmy's ear. Flexner screamed out to those who were locked in hand-to-hand struggle with Jimmy: "Get away from him. Give us space to shoot!"

They obeyed, leaping away, leaving a cleared space about Operator 5. Guns raised to blast him down.

At this moment the door to the vault room swung open, disclosing Anita Monfred in the doorway. She had a rifle at her shoulder, and it barked swiftly three times in quick succession. Three of the men who had been sighting at Jimmy Christopher were hit by those three slugs. One dropped like a sack, with a bullet through the heart. The other two screamed, and buckled over, one with a slug in his shoulder, the other with a bullet in the leg.

Anita's rifle swung about the room and she ordered coldly: "Let your guns drop to the floor!"

The courtiers dared not shoot at her. They did not know what had happened to Rudolph, did not know what she had done to him. If she had killed him, she was now their Empress. If she had not killed him, they knew that he would have no mercy for anyone who harmed her. Often in the past, they had seen her do mad things, things that would have meant Imperial displeasure and perhaps worse for anyone else; yet they had seen her restored to favor the next day, and once more in the Emperor's graces.

So these men who lived daily in abject fear of their monarch dared not shoot at the woman who might tomorrow be either their Empress or the Emperor's favorite. They let their guns drop to the floor, stood there stupidly wondering what would happen next. Flexner, too, let his weapon fall; but he murmured: "My dear Baroness! Haven't you gone too far this time?"

Anita did not answer him. Her eyes were on the figure of Jimmy Christopher, who had leaped to the vat and was lifting out his sister. Coleman and Graves quickly picked up two of the revolvers dropped by the courtiers, not understanding a thing of what was happening, but willing to take the good with the bad.

Nan had uttered one glad cry as Jimmy bent over her, and then she had sighed and closed her eyes in a dead faint. The reaction was too great. And there was a black mark on the left side of her dress, where the molten silver had already come close enough to sear.

Operator 5 lifted Nan to his shoulder and swung around. Anita called out to him: "Through here, Operator 5. Go through the vault room, and you will find a corridor to the rear entrance. There are no guards there."

Jimmy threw her a glance of thanks, headed through the vault room, with Coleman and Graves behind. They passed the vault where Rudolph lay, quiet now because he had yelled himself hoarse while the shooting was going on.

Anita called after them: "Remember your promise, Operator 5!"

Jimmy called back solemnly: "I will remember, Anita!"

Swiftly he passed through the corridor beyond, seeking the rear entrance. Coleman, immediately behind him, said in an awed voice: "Gawd! Is it going to be as easy as this?"

But it was not to be so easy.

One laboratory man dropped—as Operator 5 and Graves fired.

CHAPTER 10
OPERATOR 5 KEEPS HIS WORD

ROUNDING THE bend in the corridor, Jimmy Christopher staggered under Nan's dead weight. He glimpsed the rear door at the far end of the narrow hallway, but he also saw a small group of troopers who were rushing in their direction, aroused by the shooting.

The whole building was in fact aroused now, and cries were resounding everywhere. The troopers spied them, and uttered shouts of inquiry. They did not yet know what was the trouble, and were uncertain what to do.

It was that uncertainty on which Jimmy capitalized. He waved to the troopers with his free hand, and turned swiftly back, snapping to Graves and Coleman: "We're cut off, boys. Make for that elevator!"

There was an elevator shaft to the left, and Jimmy headed for it. The car was there and the door open. The operator was goggling at them, bewildered. He had just come down and opened his door, and having heard the shooting upstairs, he was dazed by the abrupt sight of three men in Mexican uniform, one of them carrying an unconscious girl.

Before the man could recover his wits, the three were upon him. Coleman drove a swift right to the fellow's jaw, and the man keeled over without a sound. The troopers had also rounded the bend now, and they leveled rifles, still in some doubt as to whether or not to shoot.

Jimmy stepped swiftly into the cage, and Coleman and

Graves followed him, slamming the door shut and pushing the lever far over. The cage slid upward, just as a fusillade of shots smashed the glass door of the shaft below them.

Jimmy kept Nan on his shoulder, his eyes bleak. Both the other men knew what was in his mind. Their escape was cut off now, and though they might have won a temporary respite, they were bound to be captured or killed within a very few minutes.

The cage came to a halt at the top floor, and Coleman slid open the door, pushed out with Graves behind him and Jimmy bringing up the rear, still carrying Nan.

There were no corridors on this floor. The sight that greeted their eyes was an astounding one. The entire floor space was devoted to rows and rows of benches at which white-coated men worked over retorts and test tubes. Tungsten burners glowed all over the immense area, and other men ladled a hot, muddy-colored liquid into metal containers. Still others dipped up liquid from similar containers which had already cooled, and poured them into small vials.

Men were running toward them now, led by Doctor Hugo Eckstein, the chief of the Imperial Bacteriological Warfare Division. Eckstein had a gun in his hand, and his thin features were pinched into lines of hate. But before the doctor had taken three steps, Coleman's gun blasted out at him, and he toppled backward into the arms of those behind him.

In a far corner, a man had picked up a submachine gun and raised it. Jimmy Christopher, with his free hand, snatched the gun from Graves and snapped a shot in the direction of the machine-gunner. His aim was accurate. The man dropped with a slug between the eyes.

"This way!" shouted Jimmy, and he ran with Nan on his shoulder, blasting at the massed laboratory workers with his gun. Graves picked up Eckstein's revolver on the way, and the three blazed a path to the corner where the machine gun had been dropped. Coleman seized the deadly weapon, turned and swung it in a menacing arc to cover the entire room. The laboratory workers shrank before its wicked snout.

Jimmy Christopher had spied a huge fire door opening on a staircase, and he heard the hurrying tread of many feet on those stairs. He laid Nan on the floor, raced toward that door and slammed it, placed across it the heavy iron bar that lay alongside. Now they were safe from those below—for a time at least.

Coleman and Graves grinned weakly at Jimmy. They had command of the situation with the machine gun, but they didn't just know what to do about it. "Where do we go from here, Operator 5?" Coleman demanded.

Jimmy's eyes were frantically scanning the place. They lighted on two huge coils of rope, lying alongside a painter's scaffold. He recalled having noticed that the upper part of the building was freshly painted on the outside. He pointed to the rope. "There's a way down," he said. "If there was only some place to go."

The massed laboratory workers were beginning to grow restless, trying to summon up enough courage to charge the machine gun. Battering blows smashed against the fire door from the stair well.

JIMMY WENT to the window, peered out. Down below, the

144

massed troops of the Imperial Hussars were staring up at them. There was no escape that way, even with the rope. Jimmy leaned out, and saw that to the left of the Mint Building, directly across the side street, was the old structure of the antiquated Union Hotel. His eyes lighted with speculation. "We could swing over there, but they'd meet us on the roof—"

Suddenly, his blood began to course more swiftly. On the roof of that old building, the figures of men had begun to appear. He counted them as they emerged on to the roof of the hotel—ten in all. And one of those he recognized. He could not be mistaken. He knew that wizened figure too well!

He leaned far out of the window and shouted: "Slips! Slips McGuire!"

Soldiers down below were firing up at him now, but his voice carried above the rifle shots, and little Slips McGuire recognized the voice, if he did not recognize the face. "Jimmy! Jimmy Christopher, by all that's holy! Where's Nan?"

"I've got her here. Send some of those boys down to keep the troopers out of the hotel, and stand by. We're coming over!"

Operator 5 pulled his head in, snapped orders at Graves. Coleman held the machine gun poised while Graves impressed a couple of the cowed laboratory workers for the job of dragging one of the heavy coils of rope over to the window. Then Jimmy tied one end of the rope around his waist, and clambered out on the sill.

The Hussars down below began to pepper the face of the building with rifle fire, but Jimmy calmly sought and found a foothold along the drainpipe and hoisted himself up to the roof. He removed the rope from around himself and made it fast around a smokestack, then clambered back through the window, running the gantlet of another fusillade from the street.

Coleman was still covering the crowd with the submachine gun, but Graves was at the side of the huge room, emptying his revolver into a large switchbox. He came back, grinning. "There's two more elevators over there at the other end," he said, pointing to the twin shafts in the opposite wall. "The troopers were coming up in them. I could see the indicators moving. So I shot out the switchbox, and I guess that'll kind of kill the power!"

"Good man!" Jimmy praised. "Now, heave that line over the side!"

Graves complied, and Jimmy, looking out, saw that the rope reached down to a point just above the ground-floor windows, a distance of perhaps forty feet. He measured with his eye the distance from their window to the roof of the Union Hotel, and nodded in satisfaction. "You get that swinging," he told Graves, "and you can make the roof easy. Now get. You first!"

Graves shook hands with Jimmy, said: "So long, big boy," to Coleman, and swung out of the window. Immediately the rifle fire from below increased in intensity. But Slips McGuire, MacTavish and the others on the roof of the Union Hotel had guessed the operation that Jimmy was planning, and they opened up from the hotel roof on the troopers below, driving them to cover, and giving Graves a chance to set himself swinging, pendulumlike. It was only a short distance across, and in a moment Graves had landed on the roof, caught by the willing hands of MacTavish.

"Coleman, you're next!" Jimmy ordered. "Give me that tommy gun!"

Coleman protested. "How'll you make out, Operator 5? You got your sister—"

"I'll manage," Jimmy told him shortly. "This is no time for arguments. Scram!"

Coleman gave up the submachine gun, hesitated an instant, then swung out on the rope.

Jimmy stood with his back to the window, straddling the unconscious body of Nan, moving the submachine gun in a wide arc to cover the massed laboratory workers. "Move back, all of you!" he barked. "Away over to the other end of the floor!"

They backed away from the menace of the gun, until there was a wide space between themselves and him. Now, the troopers in the stairwell outside were shooting into the fire door, and the huge iron door was beginning to give. It swayed inward, and gray-uniformed men appeared. Jimmy swung the submachine gun in that direction, sent a spray of lead screaming at them, and cut down a half-dozen. The rest backed away.

Now came what Operator 5 dreaded—but feared he must do: not the job of swinging out on the rope with Nan; not the job of facing the hail of lead from the troops below, or from other windows of the building, but….

HE TOOK from a pocket under his uniform tunic a small Mills bomb, and held it ready. Then he shouted to the massed laboratory workers, speaking their own language: "In two minutes I am going to destroy this laboratory with all its bacteria cultures. This bomb in my hand will wreck it completely. You have two minutes to get out of here!"

The men looked at him blankly for a moment, until the meaning of his words dawned on them. Then a concerted rush started for the fire door. Men crowded through that narrow doorway, twenty deep, in a frantic rush to get out before he threw the bomb. Many got through, but from the thickest of the remaining crowd came what forced Jimmy to perpetrate the slaughter he had sincerely hoped to avoid. Some of those men had revolvers, and in the press of the throng they drew them, fired at Operator 5 from behind their fellows. The shots skimmed close to Jimmy, and he tightened his lips, pulled the pin from the bomb. He had known that this was going to happen, and he hated to send these men to death.

Yet they were enemies. They were developing bacteria that would destroy America. What mercy dared he show them? He hurled the bomb.

At the same instant he stooped and heaved Nan across his shoulder, and swung out of the window. Before he was well clear of the sill, the explosion occurred.

The powerful Mills bomb rocked the floor of the building, brought down the inner walls in a mass of tangled, wrecked debris, crushing the life out of those laboratory workers who had not yet gotten through the exit. The deafening roar of the explosion deafened Jimmy, and the great blast of air fairly hurled him off the sill. He clutched wildly at the rope, seized it with one hand and swung free of the window, gripping Nan's body close to him with the other hand.

For a long moment Jimmy Christopher dangled there, with his legs twined about the rope, with Nan across his shoulder, and with enemy troopers sniping at him from cover in the street below.

Now Slips McGuire and his men on the hotel roof sent a withering barrage of lead hurtling down on the street, and the snipers became silent. Jimmy was slowly swinging, accelerating his momentum. The added weight of Nan dragged at him, threatened to cause his grip on the rope to slip. But ever and ever his arc increased. From the laboratory window behind him smoke and flame billowed in plumes, and the very building seemed to be swaying.

At last, Jimmy's foot touched the cornice of the hotel at the apex of his swing, but he failed to get a hold. He swung all the way back, and a machine gun opened up on him from somewhere below. The line of tracer bullets just missed him, but the gunner was not fast enough to follow him as he swung back on the return trip of the arc.

This time he stretched, straining every muscle of his body to catch the roof. For he knew that other machine guns would be brought into play by this time, and that another pendulum swing would result in his being shot down. As he came rushing up toward the roof he tensed, and gasped. He could see that he was going to fall short by a matter of inches!

Suddenly, as his hurtling body completed the arc close to the roof, he glimpsed the face of Sergeant MacTavish reaching over so far that the big Canadian almost fell off. Slips McGuire and two other men were holding on to MacTavish's nether extremities, and the sergeant reached out two big brawny arms and caught Jimmy Christopher's right foot!

In a moment Jimmy and Nan were over the top! Bullets slapped against the cornice, whining a chant of rage at having missed by so small a margin. And Jimmy stood up to be overwhelmed by McGuire and the others who crowded around him.

Jimmy had laid Nan down gently on the roof, and now she shuddered, a tremor went through her body, and she opened her eyes. She stared, almost unbelievingly, into the face of her twin brother, and then a wave of dread swept over her. "Jimmy! That horrid vat! The silver—"

"Quiet, Nan dearest," Jimmy soothed her. "You're out of it now. And it was—damned—close!"

MacTavish was helping Nan to her feet, and the big sergeant's face was set in hard lines. "Sure, Nan, you had no business dashing out on us that way!"

JIMMY WAS not listening. He was looking across at the Mint Building, which was now a mass of flame and wreckage. Even as he watched, the whole front wall collapsed. Men were running around wildly down below in the street, panic-stricken.

Jimmy Christopher said somberly to Slips McGuire, who had come up beside him: "Well, Slips, that's the end of the bacteria warfare. Their laboratory is destroyed."

"If only that varmint of a Rudolph was destroyed too!" Slips exclaimed bitterly.

Jimmy swung about. "We've got to get out of here, boys. This is a good time. They've stopped the machine-gun barrage.

They're too busy with the fire down there to bother with us for the minute. Let's go."

They hurried down the stairs, through the deserted old hotel. It had been evacuated for the purpose of catching these Americans, and that very evacuation served them well now in their escape, for they encountered no one until they reached the street. Here panic reigned, as crowds of uniformed guards and troopers thronged around the crashing Mint Building, watching morbidly, but keeping their distance.

A company of troopers under an officer was trotting at double-quick time toward the hotel entrance. Someone had at last thought of stopping the fugitives. The troopers glimpsed Jimmy and the others, and their officer barked a command. The troopers swung their rifles about, but before the officer could bark out the second command, Jimmy Christopher had pulled another Mills bomb from his pocket, pulled out the fuse, and hurled it.

The company of troopers disappeared in the geyserlike explosion that tore a deep crevasse in the street. Paving blocks and asphalt, blood and bones rained through the air. But the way was clear, and Jimmy shouted: "Follow me!"

He charged ahead, with the others in his wake. MacTavish, with one arm about Nan, brought up the rear. Jimmy raced around the corner, and pointed to a troop truck that was parked at the curb. Two soldiers were getting out of it, and when they saw the motley crew that raced toward them, they turned and ran.

Jimmy mounted to the cab in a leap, and threw the gearshift

into first, stepping on the starter at the same time. The others all piled into the rear, and the truck roared off down the street.

They met no further opposition until they arrived at the airport. Here, a small guard and a few mechanics were no match for the desperate Americans. In a few moments Coleman and Graves were tuning up the same plane in which they had come.

Jimmy Christopher stepped over to the radio while the others piled into the passenger compartment. Frantically he sent out the call letters for Z-7. The motors were humming, and the plane was ready to go before he got the Chief at Los Angeles. "Z-7!" he exclaimed. "I've destroyed the bacteria plant of the enemy. We need fear the cholera no longer—provided the serum we got is okay!"

Z-7's voice came back over the intervening miles of space. "It's okay, Jimmy! It's a simple chemical formula, and it's already afforded relief to thousands of victims. We're having it made in every laboratory we can rig up, and in a day or two we'll have enough of it to clear the plague out of the country!"

"Fine! I'm—glad my work is done!"

"Done? What do you mean, Jimmy?"

"Nan and Slips and the boys who were with her are leaving in a trimotored plane. Send a patrol to meet them over Rock Springs. I—won't be with them, Z-7."

"Why not?" There was a sudden tinge of suspicion in the Chief's voice.

JIMMY LOOKED around to find that Slips McGuire and Nan and the others were all watching him queerly. He steeled himself, spoke into the transmitter: "I've—got to go back, Z-7.

I gave my word to Anita Monfred that I'd surrender to her if—she helped me in a certain undertaking. She helped, Z-7, and I'm going to keep my word to her!"

"B-but, for God's sake, Jimmy, Rudolph will crucify you—"

"I'm sorry, Z-7, this is good-bye…."

There was a long silence at the other end of the ether, and finally Z-7's low voice came back. "I suppose you've got to—"

Silently, Jimmy Christopher clicked off the air. He moved away from the radio, faced the others. "You all heard," he said slowly. "I'm going back. Good-bye, Slips. Good-bye, Nan—"

Nan uttered a choked cry and threw herself into his arms. "Jimmy! You can't go. They—they'll put you in that vat—"

"You forget, dear, that there is no more vat. That building is destroyed—"

"They'll do other dreadful things to you. Jimmy—"

"I'm sorry, Nan. Don't make it too hard for me to keep my word."

He said it coldly, with finality, and Nan stood away from him, choking back a sob. Slowly, Jimmy started to leave the compartment, climbed down to the ground.

The others grouped around the doorway, watching him. Slips McGuire groaned: "Stop him, somebody, for God's sake!"

And then, across the field, they suddenly saw an automobile madly careening toward them. A good distance behind the auto they glimpsed other cars, and those others were firing at the leading car.

The careening auto came to a slithering, skidding stop close to the plane, and Anita Monfred leaped out of it. Her clothes were torn, and there was a long fresh scratch across her left cheek. She threw herself at Jimmy, exclaiming: "Quick! Stop those cars!"

Without orders from Jimmy, Slips and MacTavish leaped down and opened fire on the rapidly approaching pursuers. They got the tire of the leading car, and it swerved madly to one side, blocking the second, which skidded into it. The car behind piled into them, and the twisted wreckage of the three pursuing cars rolled over the field, bursting into flame.

Anita Monfred clung to Jimmy Christopher, looking up at him with wide eyes. "You—were coming—to give yourself up?"

Jimmy nodded. "Naturally. I gave my word."

She smiled weakly. "It—is not—necessary. I but barely escaped with my life. Rudolph was so enraged at me that he ordered me shot at once! I managed to struggle free, and here I am—a woman without a country! Will you give me sanctuary?"

Before Jimmy could reply, Nan Christopher rushed forward and folded Anita Monfred in her arms. "Of course! Come with us. I saw how you pleaded with Rudolph for me, when I was tied in the vat!"

Anita threw Jimmy Christopher a swift glance, murmured: "You are fortunate to have such a brave sister!" Then she permitted herself to be led into the plane. In a few moments they had taken off, with Jimmy Christopher at the controls, and Denver was far behind.

Operator 5 breathed a sigh of relief.

Slips McGuire was jubilant. "As soon as we get to Frisco, we each get a shot of the serum, and then we go out and give these Purple bozos hell. We'll drive 'em back to the Atlantic, by golly!"

It was at that moment that their radio came to life, and Nan took the call, listening closely for several moments. Then she said, very low: "No, he didn't go back, Z-7. Anita Monfred is with us… Jimmy is coming back to San Francisco with us."

She turned to flash a smile at Operator 5. "Yes, I'll tell him you're feeling better about that," she replied to Z-7.

Suddenly she stiffened, and listened tensely. Those near her could hear her low-voiced response. "Just sighted?" Her breath came quickly. "Yes… I understand."

Operator 5 moved closer, sudden strain in his eyes. Could it be that Diane…?—but no, Diane was safe on her way.

Nan nodded as the message poured through the air into her ears from the radio receiver. "Yes, yes. Very well, Z-7, I'll tell him."

As she turned away from the radio, her face was white and her lips were trembling.

Jimmy asked her tensely: "What's wrong, Nan?"

She raised troubled eyes to him, then spoke so that all of them could hear: "It's—something new, Jimmy. Something terrible. There's an immense fleet—powerful battleships, steaming toward San Francisco, on the Pacific. They—they're flying the—Purple flag!"

Anita Monfred exclaimed: "Of course! Rudolph has been building that fleet in Asia for months. All the labor of the East has been commandeered for it. There are one hundred capital ships, two hundred and fifty cruisers, and countless destroyers and submarines. Rudolph's ambition was to build the greatest fleet the world has ever seen, and he was planning to hurl it at your west coast as a first test. I did not know it would come so soon!"

"Good God!" exclaimed Sergeant MacTavish. "With a fleet like that, they can literally tear our coast apart! What'll we do, Operator 5?"

Jimmy laughed harshly. "What'll we do? We'll fight, Sergeant MacTavish!"

And he turned his face sternly toward the west, where the setting sun was painting the Sierras a deep blood-red.

POPULAR HERO PULPS AVAILABLE NOW:

POPULAR HERO PULPS   AVAILABLE NOW: